D1505415

THE CHRISTMAS SECRET

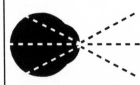

This Large Print Book carries the
Seal of Approval of N.A.V.H.

THE CHRISTMAS SECRET

DONNA VANLIERE

THORNDIKE PRESS
A part of Gale, Cengage Learning

GALE
CENGAGE Learning

Detroit • New York • San Francisco • New Haven, Conn • Waterville, Maine • London

GALE
CENGAGE Learning·

LIBRARY OF CONGRESS CATALOGING-IN-PUBLICATION DATA

VanLiere, Donna, 1966–
    The Christmas secret / by Donna VanLiere.
        p. cm. — (Thorndike Press large print basic)
    ISBN-13: 978-1-4104-2173-9 (alk. paper)
    ISBN-10: 1-4104-2173-2 (alk. paper)
    1. Single mothers—Fiction. 2. Waitresses—Fiction. 3. Department stores—Fiction. 4. Christmas stories. 5. Large type books. I. Title.
    PS3622.A66C4795 2009b
    813'.6—dc22   2009033721

Published in 2009 by arrangement with St. Martin's Press, LLC.

Printed in Mexico
2 3 4 5 6 7 13 12 11 10 09

JAN 2 6 2010

For Angela Gentry,
who gets up each day and believes

ACKNOWLEDGMENTS

Special thanks to:

Troy, Gracie, Kate, and David for game night, stick horse parades, swimming, camping, pancakes, dates with Mom at Chick-Fil-A and Jasmine, and "special nights."

Jen G., Esmond, Jen E., Sally, Sara, Matt, Tara, and Rachel Ekstrom (welcome to the team!) for your continued belief.

The folks at Meridee's and the Mercantile for great food and a spot to work.

And Mary Weekly for the blessing of your help and touching our home with grace.

7

We dance round in a ring and suppose,
But the secret sits in the middle and
knows

— Robert Frost

PROLOGUE

I didn't know my father; it's how my mother wanted it or maybe what he wanted. I don't know. I'd often find my mom staring out the kitchen window while washing the dishes at night. She always seemed to be looking for something or someone or hoping for something or someone. Her face was one of wistfulness . . . or perhaps it was longing. It's hard to recall. It changed, I suppose, from day to day.

I never asked about the man who was my father, but on my tenth Christmas I gathered my nerve as we put up our decorations. We dragged the artificial tree in from the garage and positioned the plastic Santa and reindeer on the front lawn. My heart pounded as we pulled Grandma's porcelain nativity pieces from a box of ornaments. I took a small cow from its packaging and placed it on the coffee table. I fumbled for the right words but knew I just had to come out with it. "Do you ever wish my father was here?" I asked, keeping my eyes on the bluish white cow.

She worked in silence, her hands fluttering like moths. "There was a king once," she said, peering at me over her glasses.

"Where?" I asked.

"Um," she said, polishing the shepherd boy's head with the tail of her shirt. "He lived in some far-off land. On a whim he decided to place an enormous boulder in the middle of the road."

"How'd he get it there?" I asked, lifting a lamb from the tissue paper.

She paused. "I don't know. I'm sure he had an ox move it."

"It'd take more than one ox to move a huge boulder, wouldn't it?"

She sighed, pushing her glasses up on the bridge of her nose. "He had six oxen push the boulder."

"Now that seems like too many."

"How many do you want him to have?"

I thought it over as I unwrapped the baby Jesus. "Four."

She shook her head and turned Mary just so on the table. "Okay. Four oxen moved the boulder. The king then threw buckets of water on each side of the rock so there was nothing but mud surrounding it. Then he hid himself and watched as people traveled the road. Many of his courtiers and soldiers grumbled about the enormous rock as they walked through the mud around it. Wealthy merchants and dignitaries from neighboring kingdoms complained about the king and the conditions of the roads in his kingdom yet no one would do anything about the gigantic roadblock." She added bits of straw around the nativity, pushing extra around each animal. "In time a peasant came along, carrying a sack over his back."

"What was in the sack?" I asked. "Candy?"

"Sure," she said, shoving the tissue paper back into the nativity box. "When he sees the boulder he sets his bag of candy on the ground and finds a fallen tree branch, jamming it at the base of the rock, but guess what?"

"It won't budge," I said.

"Not an inch. So he climbed on top of the branch and jumped with all his might. He jumped and jumped and jumped but . . . ?"

"Nothing," I said, picking up the baby Jesus.

"Put Jesus back on the table," she said, pointing. "Not only nothing! He fell off the branch right into that gloopy, gloppy mud. So the peasant looks all around him again and way off in the distance he sees the oxen coming his way." I picked up two wise men and pretended they were talking to each other. "Please put the wise men back down before you bust their frankincense and myrrh." She huffed at me as she lifted the figurines from my hands. "The oxen smelled that sack of candy."

My eyes bulged. "How'd they smell that small sack of candy from way far away?"

"Oxen have big nostrils," she said.

"How big?" I asked, moving Joseph closer to the action in the manger.

"Angela Christine!" I looked up at her. She had named me Angela Christine, after her mother and grandmother. She *always* called me Christine except at times like this when I exasperated her and she'd say my full name through gritted teeth.

"It doesn't matter. Would you please just listen?" She sounded like an ox sighing and went on. "The peasant harnessed the oxen together with the fallen branch and vines and in moments the boulder was moved away. To his astonishment the peasant discovered a small red velvet bag filled with gold coins and a note inside it."

I lay on the couch and threw a pillow high into the air and caught it. "What'd it say?"

She sat on the other end of the couch and

put my feet in her lap. "It said, 'Thank you for removing this boulder. Please keep this gold as a token of my appreciation. Signed, the King.' And the peasant learned what all of us learn at one time or another."

"What's that?" I asked, looking at her.

"Every rock in the road can improve our lives but we might have to get a little muddy before it does." And that's how she answered my question of if she ever wished my father lived with us.

I thought my mother had movie star looks. She had dark auburn hair she could twist on top of her head with one flick of her wrist or let hang off her shoulders, her skin was pale, and she wore tortoiseshell-framed glasses for her nearsightedness. She worked in the local bakery and would come home smelling like dough and coffee with a sack of day-old breads and pastries that had been poked by one too many old ladies looking for cream cheese filling. I often wondered what my mother would have been if she hadn't had me. I always sensed that there was another person within her as deep and beautiful as the mystery inside her heart.

There was nothing fancy about our Christmases together. With the exception of the tree, Grandma's nativity, and the plastic Santa, we didn't have any other decorations, and since there were only two of us Mom would usually bake a chicken for our meal that day with a few roasted potatoes and beans. In the days leading up to Christmas my mother would sit me down and we'd compose two letters: one to Santa that was filled with everything I could find in the JC Penney catalog and the other to God, thanking him for everything we could think of: our home; Mom's job; my stuffed bunny, Millie; Oscar, my hamster; health insurance; the money to replace the hot water heater, pay the bills, and to buy food. As I grew older the letters dwindled to one and we left it under the tree. "To remember," Mom would say. By some accounts I guess our day was pretty plain but it felt magical to me.

On those magical Christmas days with my mother I couldn't imagine any rocks in my road. I never dreamed of stumbling along without an end in sight, but when I grew up that's how I ended up living — day-to-day, survival of the fittest. I guess we're all like that in some ways. We don't dare look behind us but we're not brave enough to look ahead. We're just stuck. Right here. Waiting. I'm always waiting it seems — waiting for the right time, the right job, for the light to turn green, waiting on a call, waiting for my past to catch up with me, and for my future to begin.

I got to the point in my life where I was so tired of waiting and wanted to know that my life was not just leading *anywhere* but *somewhere*. I wanted that childhood sense of wonderment back. The crazy how, when, and why of life finally caught up with me and I realized that there was no Oz, fairy-tale king, or Scrooge waking up from a dream moment that was going to whisk me away from reality, and that's when I wanted Christmas again. The Christmas of the simple tree and polishing the nativity with my shirt-sleeve and holding my mother's hand in church. I wanted to know that there was a reason and purpose not only behind the boulder in the road but buried beneath it so that when I unearthed it I could brush off that muddy gem and say, "So this is it!" In the moment, it seemed like the wait would never end, but looking back it all passed like a misty dream.

I never moved the boulder, by the way; I couldn't. Several people helped me. Then I discovered the gift beneath it.

ONE

November — One Year Earlier

It was winter again. We were in light jackets until the week before Thanksgiving but then a gust of frigid air blew in and each day felt like deep night. Everything was cold and hard and seemed far away. While growing up, when winter grew long and weary, my mother would say, "The trees are barren and ugly now but they're rooted in the promise of spring." I understood what she was trying to say but over the years winter carried itself into summer in my life.

I walked to the door for the fourth time and looked out the window. The driveway was empty. My chest tightened and I felt pressure in my head. *Why can't a teenager ever be on time?* I wondered, crossing to my cup of coffee on the kitchen counter. I took a sip and spit it out. It had gotten cold as I waited for Allie, one of my babysitters.

"Mom, can you play with me?" my five-year-old asked, sitting on the living-room floor with two of her stuffed dogs. "Can you be Brown Dog and I'll be Genevieve?"

I crossed to the front door. "I can't right now, Haley. As soon as Allie gets here I have to bolt for work." I looked at my watch: ten fifty. I was getting angry and my face was growing pale from waiting.

"I flew again last night," Haley said, making Brown Dog soar above her head.

"In your dreams?"

"No, Mom. I got up and flew all around the house."

I kept my eye on the road. "You did that in your dreams. You fly a lot in your dreams." I noticed our neighbor's newspaper in our driveway and decided to throw it on her front porch. Mrs. Meredith looked like she was in her early seventies, and although we'd never spoken a lot, I sensed she didn't care much for my children or me. Last summer when Zach was six, he and Haley had been playing in the yard that stretches behind this row of duplexes when Zach kicked a ball that landed on Mrs. Meredith's deck, breaking her bright red hibiscus. He apologized but I don't think it helped. She wasn't used to children and I think the noise and busyness associated with them got on her nerves. To keep the peace, whenever the paperboy got a wild arm and the paper landed in my driveway, I made sure it got to her front door as soon as possible.

I scooped up the paper and walked to the front of Mrs. Meredith's house. I groaned when I heard the lock turn and looked up to see her. She was wearing a pink robe that she cinched tighter on opening the door. "Landed in my driveway," I said, holding the paper out to her. The few times we had talked Mrs. Meredith always kept the door opened about four inches as if keeping me from invading her home. I handed the paper to her through the small opening and pushed the corners of my mouth up into a faint smile.

"Thank you," she said, closing the door before I could rob her.

"You have a great day, too," I said, mumbling to myself.

Allie pulled into the driveway and I ran into the house to grab my purse. "I'm going to work, Zach," I said, craning my neck around the corner of the hall toward his bedroom. I closed the door and saw Allie sitting in her car. "Take your time," I muttered, walking to her door. "Allie, I really need you to be here at ten thirty. I can't be late to work anymore."

Her blond hair was pulled up in a scrunchy, dark liner rimmed her eyes, and big hoop earrings dangled close to her jawline. "Sorry," she said, closing her door.

I didn't have time to deal with it all again. I got in my car and sped out of the driveway, looking at my watch: ten fifty-two. "Inconsiderate kid," I said. The pressure in my head had turned into a headache and I reached back, squeezing my neck. It always felt like I was running from one place to the next, always scrambling with doubt and failure piling up inside me like snow. I sped up to make the light at Main Street but didn't make it. My heart was pounding. I couldn't be late. I prayed that the manager wouldn't notice that I wasn't there but knew it was no use. Rod had been riding me for months about being late. The disc jockey announced the time and I turned off the radio, feeling my pulse race. My nearly bald tires squealed as I turned into the parking lot the restaurant shared with the bank, and then I slammed my door, running for the back entrance. Renee was in the back prepping cups of salad dressing for the lunch rush and I glanced at the time clock: eleven thirteen. "Is Rod here?" I asked.

"He's here," Renee said, raising her eyebrows.

"Stupid sitters," I said, lining small cups of dressing onto a tray. "Did he know I wasn't here?"

" 'Fraid so, kid." Renee always called me kid even though she was no more than five years older than me.

Patterson's had been a family-owned restaurant for forty years until the last of the family died nine years earlier. No children or grandchildren wanted to leave their jobs to run a restaurant so the place was sold but the new owners kept the name. Rod was the day manager. He was in his mid-forties with a potbelly and a bald patch as wide as his forehead that ran to the back of his head. "Can you *ever* make it to work on time, Christine?"

I cringed and turned to see him behind me. "I am on time when my kids are in school. It's my sitters."

Rod scratched his domed head, looking at me. "Why aren't your kids in school now?"

"It's Thanksgiving break," I said, wrapping a fork, knife, and spoon in a napkin.

"So why were you late last week?"

My throat tightened. I didn't want to be late. It wasn't my goal each day to show up late for my job. "My five-year-old was sick and I had to find a sitter last minute."

"It's always something," he said, walking

away. Rod had been gracious throughout the summer months when I'd shown up late for work at least once a week but that cat only had so many lives and his patience was wearing thin.

I married Brad Eisley when I was twenty. Sometimes you go into a situation knowing you're making a mistake but think, "Well, I *need* a car and this one is right here and available, so how bad can it be?" Or, "The roof does need to be fixed but I *need* a house and this one is available so . . ." Brad was a nice guy, cute, and at the beginning I found him charming. We met while working at a grocery store in our hometown. I was a cashier and he stocked the shelves. He didn't work there long; he said management didn't know what they were doing. When he asked me to marry him he was unemployed; I was nineteen and consumed with the thought of being and doing nothing for the rest of my life. I was unable to go to college; my mother couldn't afford it and, although my grades had been good in high school, they weren't high enough for any sort of scholarship. There weren't a lot of men in our area so when Brad wanted to get married, I thought, "Well, he is nice and I would like to get married and he is right here asking me, so how bad could it be?"

My mother knew.

"Christine, you are a dreamer. You love books and flowers and sitting next to a lake. You need a man who will appreciate that about you. Don't marry him because you think he'll be the only one to ever ask you," she said, weeks after our engagement.

"I'm not, Mom."

"Then why are you marrying him?" she asked, folding a load of towels in the laundry room.

"He's a nice, nice guy," I said, trying to convince her as well as myself. She wouldn't look at me and that made me angry. "What's your problem with him?"

"I don't have a problem with Brad. You're right. He seems nice. I know all about nice." She stacked towels one on top of the other in silence.

I leaned against the washer and folded my arms, waiting for her to say something more. "Stop talking in code, Mom."

She placed a small stack of towels in the laundry basket and picked up another one to fold, looking at me. "Do you love him?"

"Of course I do." She nodded and continued her work. She wasn't any more persuaded than I was and that really got on my nerves.

She stopped her work. "Parents want

more for their children."

"So what's the problem? I'm getting married and that's something you never had." That hurt her and I knew it but I didn't care.

She grabbed the laundry basket and set it on her hip. "But you're not marrying the right man!"

Heat rose to my face. "I'm marrying the father of my child!"

Her face was stricken. I didn't want to tell her that way. I didn't want to tell her at all but knew my expanding belly would soon give me away. She carried the laundry past me in silence. I felt tears in my eyes but held them back. "You don't know anything about Brad," I said, my voice breaking. I grabbed my purse and left for work as she closed her bedroom door.

Months before our wedding I began to notice that Brad would demean me in front of friends and my mother and make me feel dim and irrelevant. "You don't know what you're talking about, Christy," he'd say. Or, "How dumb are you?" I married him anyway, hoping my love for him would justify any minor failings once we became man and wife. When Brad found a job here my mother seemed angry. I assumed it was because she knew that once the baby came

I would need her more than ever and she would be two hours away, but we had to move where Brad's job was.

We moved during my sixth month of pregnancy, and a month after Zach was born, Brad promptly lost his job. "Management didn't know what they were doing," he said, the veins in his neck swelling. Brad knew so much more than anyone else. He'd yell at the sportscasters and television news anchors; his jaw hanging open so wide I could see his lungs flapping for breath. Employers never knew what they were doing and I was a constant disappointment. I didn't tell my mother he lost that job and when I discovered we were having another baby I found myself making up a job title for him so she'd think he worked and earned more than he did. I didn't tell her when the electricity was turned off twice in one winter, when Brad wrecked the car and we didn't have insurance to get it fixed, or when he left less than two and a half years later. Marriage and fatherhood wasn't what he thought it would be.

He'd been gone for two months before I could build up the nerve to tell her. Haley was six months old and needed antibiotics and I was broke so I called Mom. She didn't say I told you so. She asked about the kids and my job but didn't talk much. She'd said it all before I got married and there wasn't anything left to say. I couldn't undo my mistakes. When I was a child I dreamed of a life that would be extraordinary. After I married Brad I hoped for one that was at least interesting and when I ended up alone with two kids I groped for one that was somehow manageable. That's how dreams go sometimes.

I finished my shift and clocked out; staying until seven twelve to make up for the time I missed that morning. Renee and the other waitresses had left for the day and the new shift had arrived. I tried to make a quick getaway before Rod saw me.

"Christine, you can't be late anymore." I stopped and turned to see him stepping out of the walk-in cooler. "We get way too busy during the holidays. This is your last warning."

I nodded. "See you tomorrow, Rod."

Jason Haybert pulled a five dollar bill out of his wallet and handed it to the stewardess. "Rum," he said, folding the newspaper.

She ran her tongue over her teeth. He was one of those young bucks who made a big deal out of drinking on an airplane, dying to prove that he was of age. "ID please," she said, sizing him up. *Twenty-two or twenty-three,* she thought to herself. He handed her his driver's license and she smiled. "Oh, you just had a birthday. Happy twenty-four!" He poured the rum into his cup of cola and handed the empty bottle back to her.

"Maybe when we land I can take you out for a drink."

She blushed, laughing. "I think my husband and children might have a problem with that."

"Bring them, too," he said.

She cackled and pushed her cart to the next seat. Jason had inherited his father's sandy brown hair and blue eyes, had been one of the university's best soccer players, and he thought one of the most valuable employees at the accounting firm until they downsized and gave him the boot. He was confident another equally impressive firm would snap him up before the dust settled on his desk, but three months later he still couldn't find a job. He took the call from his grandfather half-seriously.

"Come work for me at the store for the Christmas season," his grandfather Marshall had said three weeks earlier.

"Grandpa, I went to college for a reason," Jason had said. He hadn't intended that to sound so demeaning.

"How are you making money right now?"

Jason clicked the remote to the sports channel. "I'm not," he had said, reading the day's highlights on the screen.

Marshall couldn't imagine sitting around and not working when there were bills to pay. "So how are you paying rent?" he had asked. Jason was quiet. "Fly here this weekend and check it out. Once you find a job you'll be out of here. But in the meantime, you'll make some money."

Jason paused. His skills were above working at a department store but one firm after another said they weren't doing any hiring until the New Year. He didn't go to college to sell socks to old ladies but it seemed his grandfather's offer was the best thing going right now.

Marshall Wilson pressed his nose closer to the pictures in the catalog. "What are those flowers?" he asked the florist. "Those are pretty."

"Lisianthus," she said.

"Never heard of them." He flipped through the pages. "How about those?"

She leaned over the counter to see the picture. "Casablanca lilies."

Marshall rubbed the whiskers on his chin.

"Those are nice. Can I see one in person?"

"Well, no," she said. "It's the wrong time of year for lilies."

"Where?"

"What?" she said, flustered.

"Where is it the wrong time of year for lilies?" He set the book on the counter, looking at her.

"Here."

"But it could be the right time of year in another part of the world?"

She thought for a moment. "Sure . . . but it would be very expensive to buy them and —"

"Can we put some of those first flowers in there, too? What were they called? Lis something."

"Lisianthus. But again that's not an average flower and —"

"Save your breath, Natalie," Dwight Rose said, stepping beside her. Dwight had owned Rose's Floral and Gift for fifteen years. "What is it, Marshall? Anniversary or birthday? I get them confused."

"Anniversary," Marshall said, thumping his hand on top of the counter. "Number forty-four coming up in December."

"Marshall married a very sensible woman," Dwight said. "She never wanted big gems, gaudy necklaces, or, these are her words, 'ridiculous hoopy earrings.' Just flowers. Nothing fancy or exciting per se. All the reasons she married Marshall."

Marshall bowed. "Thank you, sir. I will take that as a compliment of the highest order."

"But Marshall doesn't like simple flowers. He likes to pick ones he's never heard of before. It makes him feel —"

"Less simple," Marshall said, smiling.

"Linda realized many years ago that between Thanksgiving and Christmas she was in essence a widow." Marshall rolled his eyes. "She'd make dinner but Marsh here would still be at the store and wouldn't show up until after ten o'clock each night."

"It was never ten o'clock," Marshall said.

"Okay, eleven," Dwight said. Marshall sighed and waved his hand in the air to hurry Dwight along. "Linda decided that she'd take this time to travel the country and visit the kids and grandkids. After —"

"A few weeks away came the long-awaited return and a bouquet of beautiful flowers," Natalie said, finishing his sentence. "That's so romantic." She pulled the pages of flowers out of the catalog.

Dwight put his hand on the young woman's back. "No one, not even Linda, has ever referred to Marshall as romantic."

"You have no idea what goes on behind closed doors," Marshall said, picking up the photos.

"Great. Now I'll have that image in my head all day," Dwight said.

Marshall laughed and tucked the pages in his jacket pocket. "I'll run these by Judy and get back with you." He thumped the top of the counter and walked out the door, heading down the street to Wilson's Department Store. He and Linda opened Wilson's four years after they got married and it had since been a mainstay on the town square. Once their first child started to toddle about the store, Linda decided to stay at home where she raised two more children.

Twenty-five years earlier doctors had removed one of Linda's breasts. When the cancer showed up in her colon a few months later, Linda went in for her second surgery in less than a year. The chemotherapy, radiation, and medications left her weak and sick and Marshall didn't step foot in Wilson's for three months straight. "Go, Marshall," Linda would say.

"The store is in fine hands," Marshall had said. He knew she wanted a break from his constant hovering, but the thought of losing her gripped him stronger than anything he'd ever felt. He planned trips overseas for he and Linda and bought her necklaces, rings, and a diamond tennis bracelet.

"Oh, Marsh," she had said when she opened it. "I don't need this."

"I want you to have it," he said, sitting on the edge of the bed.

She smiled. "I know you do," she said, slipping her hand into his. "But you don't have to buy me expensive gifts to make me think you love me any more now that I'm sick. You haven't stepped foot into the store in months. I *know* you love me."

"But I've never gotten you anything like this."

She squeezed his hand. "I've never needed anything like this. I've been very happy with you without a bracelet like this and I'm quite certain I'll still be just as happy." He leaned down and kissed her forehead. "I'm not going anywhere," she whispered.

He settled for buying Linda flowers and when she recovered and was cancer-free he sent her a fresh bouquet every week and for any occasion over the years.

Marshall swung open the office door. "Have you ever heard of lisianthus, Judy?" He threw the catalog pages on her desk and stepped up to his office, hanging his jacket on the coatrack.

"It's a virus, right?" Judy asked, flipping through files in the cabinet.

"It's a flower," he said.

She stepped over to her desk and peered at the catalog pages over her glasses. "Pretty," she said. Judy Luitweiler had worked for Marshall for twenty-seven years and in that time all of her children had grown up, married, and produced six grand-children. Judy had started out on the sales floor but soon became Marshall's right-hand man in the office.

"Would you like it?" Marshall yelled from his office.

Judy pulled a file from the bottom drawer and opened it. "I'd love it. But I never claimed to have a favorite flower, either."

He stepped to the door. "Don't you think hydrangeas get kind of old after a while?"

"I'm just saying," she said.

He started to close his office door behind him. "Have you heard anything from Jason?"

She took a bite of a powdered donut and brushed the powder off her sweatshirt. "Not yet. I'm sure he'll come directly here from the airport." She took another bite and tapped her index finger on the desk to clean up the powder, licking it off, and making yummy noises. "Are you sure you're up for this?"

He stuck his head around the corner to look at her. "Up for what?"

She took a sip from her "My Grandma's the Best" coffee mug. "A visit from Jason? He's never been your favorite grandchild."

"How would you know who is and isn't my favorite?"

"I know," she said, shoving the last bite into her mouth.

Marshall grunted and closed his door.

Jason pulled out his cell phone and hit speed dial. "Hey, babe," he said, looking out the window of the taxi. "I'm here."

"I still can't believe you're doing this," Ashley said. Jason had met Ashley during their senior year of college and they had dated on and off for the past three years. His parents found her remote and cool as stone but were kind to her for his sake. Ashley was pretty, thin, opinionated, and talented. She worked for a fashion designer in the city and wanted to design her own clothing line someday. Trouble was, her depth ran as deep as fabric blends and colors. Theirs was a relationship of pleasure and convenience.

"Why don't you come back to the city?

Plenty of firms will need you," Ashley said.

"Firms are letting people go," Jason said. "Not hiring them."

The taxi driver made his way through the town square and Jason watched as they passed familiar sights from his childhood. Jason's mother was the oldest of Marshall and Linda's children and the one most like her mother. Although she was forty-three Marshall usually called her Bunny. "My parents used to bring me and my sister to our grandparents each summer for two whole weeks," Jason said into the phone. He shook his head. "Now I can't imagine staying here for two weeks let alone through the Christmas season." He groaned out loud. "I'll call later." He snapped the phone closed and slipped it into his pocket. Jason had a great sense of self-importance about him. He was college-educated; his grandfather was not. He had traveled the world through college; his grandparents had always loved their hometown and the people in it. He aspired for more.

Jason paid the taxi driver and lifted his bags from the trunk. He opened the front door of Wilson's and pulled his suitcase behind him. A slim young girl with blond curly hair looked up from behind a rack of clothing. "Good morning," she said, much too perky for Jason. "Can I help you find anything?"

"Marshall Wilson," he said, unzipping his jacket.

The salesgirl looked at the suitcase and threw her hands in the air. "Oh! You're Jason. He's been looking for you. The office is that way at the back of the store."

Jason readjusted his backpack and looked at his suitcase. "Can you bring that for me?"

"Sure," she said, pulling the suitcase behind her. "I'm Debbie, by the way. I work in ladies' clothing."

Jason took the stairs by two up to the office and rapped on the window.

"He's here!" Judy yelled over her shoulder toward Marshall's office. She opened the door and threw her arms around Jason's neck. "Look at you, Mr. Handsome!"

Marshall stepped beside Judy and hugged Jason to him. "So good to see you, Jace." He noticed Debbie attempting to drag the suitcase up the stairs. "Let me get that." He carried it up the stairs and set it outside the office door.

Jason threw his backpack on one of the chairs opposite Judy's desk and sat on the other one.

"So how was your trip?" Marshall asked, preparing a cup of coffee for him.

"Great. The flight was actually on time." Marshall handed him the cup and Jason grimaced after taking a sip.

"How's Ashley?" Marshall asked.

"Awesome. We broke up for a while but now we're back together, I think."

"You think?" Marshall asked.

"We're up and down. Hot and cold." He opened his phone and showed a picture to Judy.

"How gorgeous," she said, leaning forward. "What does she do?"

"She wants to work in the fashion industry."

Judy bugged out her eyes to look impressed.

"Maybe she could come here and help our buyers," Marshall said. "Be good experience."

Jason laughed. "Anybody can be a buyer, Grandpa. She wants to design." He slipped his phone into the backpack. "Hey, I know you said I could stay at the house but I think it'd be easier in a place of my own."

Marshall sat on the edge of Judy's desk. "But a place would be hard to find and would cost —"

"Already found one online," Jason said, setting his coffee down. "Paid the first month's rent."

Marshall nodded. "Where?"

"It's a garage apartment owned by a guy named Robert Layton."

"I had no idea Robert and Kate rented an apartment."

"They said I'm only the second renter. So," Jason said, stretching, "did you want me in here doing the books or is there an office somewhere else?"

Judy cleared her throat and busied herself with wiping dust from her computer screen.

"Judy keeps the books," Marshall said. "I want you on the floor."

Judy cleaned pencil shavings and gum wrappers from her top drawer and straightened the paper clips.

"I thought you wanted me for accounting work through the holidays."

Marshall shook his head. "No. Judy does that. I need help on the floor through Christmas."

"Then why did you ask me to come help with the books?"

Judy cleaned the rim of her coffee mug with a tissue.

"I didn't," Marshall said.

"But that's what I heard you say," Jason said.

"You heard wrong."

Jason stood and threw his backpack over

his back. "I'm kind of overqualified for floor work, Grandpa."

Judy leaned over to tie her shoe.

"I agree," Marshall said. "But you need money."

Jason looked at the floor, then to Marshall. "I'm not sure if this will be a good fit."

Judy untied her other shoe and worked at retying it.

"Suit yourself," Marshall said. "You know you're welcome here. Let me know what you decide."

Jason nodded and opened the office door. "See you, Judy."

Judy leaned up and waved both hands in the air. "Bye-bye, handsome!" Jason closed the door and Marshall and Judy watched him through the large window as he dragged the suitcase down the stairs and through the main aisle of the store. "Well, you're off to a great start," Judy said, slapping Marshall's shoulder.

He turned to step back up to his office. "How many shoes do you have under that desk, anyway?"

"It was *awkward!*" she said, yelling at his back.

I drove up to our duplex and noticed that every light was on in the place. I walked in and flipped off the light in the entry and around the corner in the hall. Allie was sitting on the sofa, watching television. "Hi, Allie." I crossed the living room and threw my purse on the kitchen table. The place was a mess and I tried to hide my frustration. "How were the kids?"

Allie stood and gathered her things. "Great. I can't come tomorrow, Christine."

"What? I asked you weeks ago if you could work and you said yes."

"I know but my mom wants to take us to a huge outlet mall an hour away to start shopping for Christmas."

I felt a pain at the back of my head. "I don't know anyone else to call. That's why I set this up with you a long time ago."

She opened the door. "I'm really sorry. My mom said it's the only day she can take us before Christmas."

She closed the door and I yanked open the kitchen drawer, pulling out wads of coupons and miscellaneous notes. "I *cannot* believe this!" I said, yelling up to the ceiling. I swore at that moment that I'd never use Allie again but I knew my hands were tied. A stack of bills sat by the phone and I flung them to the floor. I couldn't even bear the sight of them. I found the scribbled note I was looking for and dialed the number.

"Hi, Elaine, this is Christine Eisley. We met at Patterson's when you came in a few weeks ago."

"Oh, sure, hi," she said.

"You said to call you if I ever needed your daughter to babysit and I need someone at ten thirty in the morning."

"I'll check with her and have her call you back."

I hung up and tried to take a deep breath. I stepped back onto a stuffed toy and kicked it out of the way. "Zach! Haley!"

"Coming," Zach said.

I waited a second but didn't hear the bedroom door open. "Now, now, now!" I shouted, storming into the living room. "Get out here right now!" I hated myself for taking my anger out on them. Zach and Haley ran down the hall to the living room and I pointed at the toys on the floor. "Put all of these away."

Haley held up her stuffed dog to me. "Genevieve did it."

"I don't care who did it," I said, my voice quivering. "Get these toys out of here!"

They started to gather the toys in their arms and carry them down the hall. I wanted to go to them and apologize for yelling but I couldn't. I was frustrated and weary and unable to move. Time and again

I find myself fighting and scraping to keep my head above water and have been ready to give the whole thing up. I have told myself that the kids would be better off somewhere else with someone who can provide everything they need. I am barely equipped to take care of myself, let alone two other people whose lives depend on me. I have questioned if I am doing the right thing or making the best decisions. So many times I have felt like a babe in the woods the way I kept getting lost on the wrong roads, and my bad decisions still affected me . . . and my kids. They deserved better. I knew that. The doorbell rang and I moved to the door, trying to peer out the window. I could see the top of a man's head but didn't know who it was.

"Hello," I said through the door.

"Christy." I stopped at the sound of his voice. Brad always called me Christy and I detested that name.

My jaw tightened. What was he doing here? I did *not* want to deal with him right now. "What?"

His tone was kind. "Could you open the door?"

I yanked it open and stepped out onto the porch, closing the door behind me before the kids heard anything. I had left my coat inside and folded my arms to keep warm. Brad hadn't shaved in days and dark brown hair spread over his face. He was wearing a gray knit cap and a denim jacket with black motorcycle boots. He tried hard to look cool but it never worked for him. "What are you doing here?"

"I want to see the kids."

"Then pay child support." I was so sick of this same conversation.

"I'm supposed to see them this weekend."

"Technically, yes," I said, keeping my voice low so the kids wouldn't hear. "But there's that issue of child support again."

He smiled. "Come on, Christy. They're my kids."

I hated his tone and his smile and the smell of his aftershave. "If you had any desire to see those kids you'd do everything in your power to provide for them but you don't. I provide for them, Brad. Me!" I was shivering and turned to go back inside.

"Um, I called earlier and some little girl told me you were working late. I asked if the kids had eaten and she said no. Have they eaten anything yet?"

I hated him. My mother constantly told me not to talk to him. "You do *not* have to talk to him," she would say. "Don't answer the door or pick up the phone." My back broke out in perspiration and I turned to look at him.

"Your hours bother me," he said. "I just don't see how it's possible to take care of our children."

Something pressed hard against my chest. "They stopped being *our* children when you walked away!" I said. I realized I was shouting and I lowered my voice again.

I could see him smiling and he lit a cigarette. "This isn't right. A little girl shouldn't be raising our children."

Brad was constantly taking me back into court for any reason. Tears burned my eyes. I had learned a long time ago that no one was home in his soul. I stepped closer to him. "Don't threaten me! Don't you even threaten me!"

"Don't you try to keep my kids from me." He turned his back to me and walked toward his car.

"You haven't paid a dime in six months. I don't have to let them see you."

I heard him laugh. "Yes, you do," he said.

I stepped inside the house and slammed the door. When I was a little girl I wanted to get married, become a teacher, have children, and live out my days in a sweet, perfect little house where joy rang out from the walls. Dreams like that die hard.

"What's wrong, Mom?" Haley asked, standing in the hallway. Zach was next to her. I couldn't answer. Words lodged in my throat.

"Mom, are you mad?" Zach asked.

My breath was shallow and I could feel the heat in my face. "Yes," I said, falling into the sofa.

"At us?" Zach asked. I shook my head. "Something happen at work?"

I shook my head again. "Go get ready for bed," I said, trying to find my voice.

"I'm hungry," Haley said.

I looked up at her and tried to smile. "Get ready for bed, then come out for something."

"Can we eat first?" Zach asked.

I spoke through my teeth. "Zach, don't argue with me tonight." I heard them turn and tiptoe down the hall. Tears dripped on to my hands. It was too much. The boulder in the road was getting bigger every day.

Two

Jason walked the few blocks to Wilson's that morning. After making a call to his head-hunter he knew there wasn't an accounting job on the horizon. He'd just have to suck it up and work "on the floor" for a few weeks. Jason opened the front door and his feet slipped beneath him. "Careful!" Debbie shouted, trying to block the watery path. "We've sprung a leak."

Jason looked above him. "That's a lawsuit waiting to happen."

"I've tried to call for maintenance but my intercom isn't working up here. Would you mind telling them that I need help?"

Jason walked to the office and threw open the door. Judy waved her hands in the air and clapped them together. "So is it official? Are you on the clock?"

"I guess so," he said.

Marshall stepped down from his office. "Judy, could you show Jason where the time clock and break room are?"

Jason flinched. He'd never thought of himself as a time clock kind of guy. Judy brushed crumbs of pastry off her "Happiness Is a Hug from your Grandchild" sweatshirt and banged her hands together again. "Isn't this exciting? Come on, handsome."

She opened the door and Jason looked back at Marshall. "Oh. Some lady at the front needs help. The roof is leaking."

"Not again," Judy said, crossing to the phone. "Which lady was it, love?"

Jason thought for a moment. "The one at the very front of the store."

"Was it the woman who helped with your suitcase yesterday?" Marshall asked.

"I think so," Jason said.

Marshall rolled his eyes at Judy. How difficult was it to recall if it was the same woman? Judy called maintenance for help and led Jason out of the office and down the stairs toward the break room. "Everyone clocks in here," she said, pushing open the door to an empty room filled with vending machines and three small round tables with chairs. She handed him his card.

He took the card and punched in for the day, hating the sound the machine made. "How have you done this for twenty-seven years, Judy?"

"I stopped clocking in twenty-six years ago," she said, laughing. He followed her out of the room and up the stairs. "You'll be working in menswear today. Matt is the floor supervisor and he'll help you out." She led him into the department and waved at a man standing in front of a mannequin that was dressed in jeans and a sweater.

"Is that the floor supervisor?" Jason asked. "How old is he?" He was annoyed at the thought of answering to someone his age or younger.

"I'm not sure. He's married with a little boy." She clapped Jason on the back. "Jason, this is Matt."

Matt extended his hand. "Marshall's told me all about you. Glad you can help out."

Judy blew a kiss in the air toward both of them. "I'm headed out for supplies. You boys be good!"

Jason's phone buzzed and he pulled it out of his pocket to read the text message. He smiled and put it back in his pocket.

"Text message?" Matt asked.

Jason nodded. "From my girlfriend. Well, sort of my girlfriend."

"Phones aren't allowed on the sales floor," Matt said, walking toward a display. "Marshall has no patience for texting or cell phones in general."

"I don't think he'd mind if I sent a quick text here and there," Jason said.

Matt laughed, shaking his head. "Whatever you say," he said. "Why don't you work on stripping all of the displays in this department? New clothes are laid out on the counter there for each one." Jason watched him talk. Did he just ask him to strip down a mannequin? Jason turned to see the pile of clothes. "When you're done with that," Matt said, "there's lots of inventory we need to unload in the back."

Jason stepped to the first mannequin and unzipped the jeans. He couldn't believe what he was doing.

Elaine's daughter Mira arrived right at ten twenty-five. I opened the door and she leaned down toward Haley, smiling. "Hi, Haley! Are you ready to play?" I loved her!

"They can have mac and cheese for lunch," I said, slinging my purse over my shoulder. "Don't let them eat a bunch of junk. There's some grapes, apples, and cheese in the fridge. Or peanut butter's in the cabinet next to the stove." I yelled down the hall toward Zach's bedroom, "Mira's here, Zach, and I'm headed to work." I kissed Haley and walked out to my car.

I turned the key and put the car in reverse

when I saw a vehicle come to a stop at the end of the driveway. "What are you doing?" I said to myself, watching the car. I waited a moment but the car stayed there, blocking my driveway. "Come on!" I shouted, looking out the back window. I honked my horn and waited. I honked again and inched my car closer to the car so the driver could take the hint. Obviously, the driver didn't get the point at all. I threw my car in park and jumped out. As I walked around the front of the driver's car I could see it was a woman and she was slumped onto the steering wheel. For a brief moment I wondered if it was someone pulling a prank. I tapped on her window. "Hey!" I shouted. "Hello!" My heart raced and I knocked louder. She didn't move.

I opened her door and reached out to touch her shoulder. "Ma'am," I said. I found myself shouting at her. "Are you okay?" Her head flopped back on the driver's headrest and my body jerked in response. I ran for my car and threw open the door, grabbing my purse. I fumbled through it looking for my phone before dumping the contents on the driveway. Where were the other cars on the road? Why was it so quiet? Where was Mrs. Meredith? She was always home! I snatched up the phone, flipping it open. It slipped out of my hand onto the concrete and the battery snapped off and slid under my car. "Oh, God," I said, trying to reach the battery. "I need help here," I said, scrambling to my feet. I couldn't run for the house; it would take too much time. "Mira!" I screamed, hoping she'd hear me. I reached the woman's door and pulled her from the car. I could hear my heart in my ears as I fumbled for the pulse on her neck. "Ma'am," I said, shaking her shoulders. I hadn't done CPR since health class in high school and my hands shook. I tilted her head back and began chest compressions. "Help me," I said, pressing my mouth to hers.

Mira saw me from the living-room window and ran to my side. Haley and Zach were close behind. "Go!" I screamed, waving my arm. "Call for help and keep the kids in the house." I continued chest compressions and the woman gasped for air. My heart boomed through my chest. "Someone's coming," I said. My voice was ragged and thin. Her eyes remained closed and she reminded me of my grandmother.

"What happened?" she said, whispering.

I took off my jacket and put it under her head. "I don't know. You stopped breathing."

Her eyes fluttered open and she squinted at me in the sun. "Where am I?"

"You're in front of my house."

"I'm so sorry," she whispered.

I pulled her jacket tighter around her. "Don't apologize. I'm grateful you're breathing again."

She attempted a smile. "So am I. What's your name?"

"Christine," I said.

She tried to find my hand and I slid it into hers. "You're a waitress?"

"Yes."

"I was a waitress once," she said. "It's how I met my husband." Her hand lost its strength and began to slide from mine. "Will you stay with me?"

My mind raced. My shift started at eleven. "Yes," I said, glancing down the street. I could hear the ambulance making its way through town. She lay still with her eyes closed and I shivered as a breeze swept across the sweat that stood on my back.

"My car," she said. "It's in your way."

"Don't worry. I'll move it," I said. I worried that she wouldn't remember where she had been driving when she blacked out. "I can take it to your home or work or wherever. Where do you work?" Her eyes were closed and I wasn't sure if she heard me.

"Downtown," she said, so low I had to strain to hear her.

"I can leave it in front of Patterson's and the keys under the mat." She squeezed my hand. The ambulance grew louder and I looked down at her. "It's almost here," I said.

The ambulance stopped in the middle of the road and a man and a woman jumped from the back, rushing to the woman's side. I moved out of the way and watched as they checked her vital signs and spoke to her. "Do you know her?" the man said, turning to me.

"No," I said, wrapping my arms tight around me.

"What happened?" They were putting her on top of a collapsible stretcher.

"I don't know," I said. "I found her slumped over the wheel of her car." They raised the stretcher and moved it toward the back of the ambulance. I ran for her car and lifted her purse off the front seat. "This is hers," I said, handing it to the paramedic inside the ambulance. "For ID. Tell her family that I'll park her car at Patterson's Restaurant. Keys under the mat." They closed the doors and I watched as they drove away. I was trembling.

I picked my jacket up off the ground and

threw the contents of my purse back inside it. I had five minutes to get to work. My heart was still racing as I sped through town and I hoped that Rod wouldn't notice that I was late. I parked the woman's car in front of the restaurant and slipped in the front door, scanning the place for Rod. I put my jacket and purse in the cabinet under the cash register. Renee caught my eye and moved her hand across her forehead. It was five after eleven but I had made it. She pointed to a section at the back of the restaurant and I grabbed an ordering pad. I smiled at a couple who were looking over the menu and approached their table to greet them. "Hi," I said.

"Renee's got this section, Christine." I turned to see Rod walking toward me.

"Oh, she thought I was back here," I said.

"No," he said, motioning for me. "You're done. Gather your things. I'll have your final check on Monday."

My stomach dropped. "What? Why, Rod?"

His forehead turned red. "I told you that if you were late one more time that that would be it."

"A lady passed out at the end of my driveway," I said, following him through the restaurant. "I had to give her mouth-to-mouth."

He didn't believe me. "Sorry, Christine."

I pointed to the front of the restaurant; my hands were shaking. "Her car is right out there. She's in the hospital and I said I'd park her car here so her family could get it."

He turned to look at me. "Best of luck."

He walked past me and I rubbed the sweat off my upper lip. I ran after him, grabbing his arm. "Rod, I need this job. You know I do."

He pulled his arm from me. "Lots of people need jobs. Some people actually work when they get one."

An image of Brad raced through my mind and my eyes filled. I could *not* lose this job. He would use it against me and try to get primary custody. Rod had to know how desperate I was. "Please, Rod. This was not my fault. I had to help that woman."

Renee overheard us and stepped next to Rod. "We're so busy," she said. "Can't you give her another chance?"

He wouldn't look at her. "Gather your things, Christine." He walked into the office and closed the door.

Renee balanced the tray she was carrying on her hip and leaned in to hug me. "I'm so sorry, kid."

I nodded and my legs shook as I walked

toward the crowd of customers who were waiting for a table. The other two waitresses formed what they could of a smile as I picked up my purse and jacket from under the hostess station and moved through the waiting area to the front door. I pushed it open and a rush of something like sadness or injustice or disbelief filled my throat and when I stepped onto the side-walk I shoved my jacket to my mouth, sobbing.

"Are you okay, miss?" I glanced up to see an older man in front of the restaurant and turned my head away from him, nodding. "Are you sure? I can take you into the store and get you some help."

I shook my head and walked away, hoping he wouldn't say anything else. I turned into the alley between the restaurant and the bank and waited for him to walk away. It took a few seconds before I heard him leave. I peered around the corner and watched as he waved at someone on the street before going into Wilson's.

The phone on Marshall's desk rang about twenty minutes after eleven. He hung it up and hurried toward the entrance of the store. "What's wrong?" Jason asked as he and Matt kept in step behind him.

"Judy's unconscious in the hospital!" He

and Jason jumped into Marshall's green Dodge Stratus and pulled out of the lot.

I realized I had driven the woman's car to the restaurant and I didn't have a ride home. Tears burned my eyes and I pulled a tissue from my purse, pressing it to my face. This was what I got for helping someone. I looked up and down the street, for what I don't know, and started walking in the direction of the bus station. The air made me shiver and I stopped to put on my jacket before crossing the road. I pulled up the zipper and stepped off the curb, jumping as a green car laid on its horn and raced by me. For a brief second I wished it would have hit me and cried harder. Why couldn't anything ever go right? Why was everything always so hard? The bus station was eight blocks away but it didn't feel like my legs could carry me there. I passed the florist and the flowers in the window caught my eye. They were beautiful pink and blue and white hydrangeas, my favorite. Brad never gave me flowers. Not even once. He said they died and were a waste of money.

I wanted to call someone and tell them what had happened but I didn't know who that would be. My mother and her husband Richard were out of town visiting his parents and I didn't want to bother them. Mom had always prided herself on never asking anyone for help when she was raising me; I was her responsibility and she took care of me on her own. I had fallen in step right behind her, failing to even call her when I needed help.

I'll figure it out, I said to myself, shoving the tissue inside my jacket pocket. The sign for the bus station was visible in the distance and I picked up my pace. I stopped at the corner of Main and Fourth Street and waited for the light to turn green before I crossed the road.

"Excuse me."

I turned to see a woman with light brown hair that hung to her shoulders in a wispy mess. She looked to be in her midthirties but something in her eyes seemed much older. I had been a waitress since I was seventeen years old and had seen a lot of faces over the years. Every once in a while I really see what's in those faces, something that stops me. I can't describe it exactly but it's something there in the eyes or in the lines on the upper lip or across the forehead that reveals unexpected pain or beauty or both and in that split second of a moment my heart breaks for that person. I don't know what it was about the woman in front of me — maybe it was how close her skin stuck to her bones or the dark circles that cast moonlike shadows under her brown eyes. Whatever it was, I felt like I needed to protect her, defend her, or take her home.

"I'm looking for Daley's. Do you know where that is?"

I thought for a moment. "Is that the truck stop?"

She shrugged and held up the classified section of the newspaper. "I don't really know. They need a cashier."

She looked breakable; there was no way I was going to send her to Daley's. "You don't want to work at the truck stop," I said. "They'll put you on the night shift and the smoke will kill you." She nodded without looking at me. "Hey, why don't you go to Patterson's? I know they need a waitress."

She glanced up at me. "I don't think I'd make a very good waitress."

"Then you'd be perfect for Patterson's." I turned around and pointed up the street. "It's up that way about six blocks, right next to the bank and Wilson's. While you're up that way you should apply at Wilson's, too."

"No matter what you're going through," my mother would say as I was growing up, "someone else has it worse." I watched as the woman walked away and knew, without knowing anything about her, that her life was a bigger mess than mine.

I turned to head for the bus stop again when I noticed people mingling on the sidewalk off Fourth Street, waiting for a table at Betty's Bakery and Restaurant. I realized I had forgotten about that little restaurant tucked away off the main drag in town. I pulled out my compact and fixed the black lines under my eyes and put on fresh lipstick.

The lunch crowd stood outside the doors and filled the small waiting area. I pressed through them and the smell of cinnamon and hazelnut filled the restaurant. A waitress was filling a customer's glass with water. Unlike Patterson's, Betty's didn't have the newest furnishings. The chairs were hardwood or wicker-backed, the floors were dark, knotty pine, two walls were exposed red brick and old newspaper articles and magazine covers were hung on them. Blue and white checkered cloths draped each table and baskets hung from the ceiling. The front counter curved from one end of the restaurant to the waitress station, enclosing the short-order prep area where sandwiches, soups, and salads were made. The first third of the counter was wooden and covered with Betty's T-shirts and sweatshirts for sale along with bags of coffee beans. The remaining two-thirds of the counter was glass that looked down into a brightly lit display of cakes, pies, pastries, bread, and cookies that stretched back to the waitress station. Across from the display cabinets were three wooden racks filled with day-old and fresh bread and rolls. It smelled like the bakery where my mother used to work. "Excuse me," I said to the waitress. "Is there a manager on duty?"

She glanced at my Patterson's uniform. "Are you going to work or looking for work?"

"I'm looking," I said. "Are you hiring?"

"I hope so," she said, pointing to the back. "Betty Grimshaw's the owner. She's the lady with gray hair, talking to those people at the four-top."

I walked through the maze of tables and waited for Betty to finish her conversation. Something about this place felt so different from Patterson's. Betty turned toward me, looking at my uniform. "You showed up for work at the wrong restaurant," she said.

I faked a laugh and stuck out my hand. "Hi, Betty. I'm actually looking for work. I'm Christine."

Betty Grimshaw had opened Betty's on her own twenty-five years ago. It started as a small bakery and grew to include the restaurant. She was short and plump, wore glasses on a chain around her neck, and cackled when she laughed. She studied me and then motioned with her head for me to follow her. "How long have you been at Patterson's?"

"Just over a year and a half," I said, weaving in and out of tables.

"A long-termer," she said, stepping into the kitchen. "It's a revolving door down there." I didn't say anything. She pointed to a young woman working with dough. "Don't handle that too much, Stephanie. If you work the dough too much it won't be flaky. It's ready now." Stephanie floured the table and rolled the dough out in front of her. A timer buzzed and Betty opened the oven, pulling out a large tray filled with pastries. "Stephanie, give these a few minutes but then use that pastry bag and drizzle icing over each one. And don't be stingy with it. No one's watching their weight when they eat one of these and they expect it to be fabulously gooey." Betty washed her hands in the sink and dried them with a paper towel. "Do you cook, or bake, or wait tables, Christine?" She stepped out of Stephanie's way and leaned against the walk-in refrigerator. I wondered how old she was; her hair was a soft white with a few streaks of pepper throughout, some would say her moon face was half-ruined with lines but I thought it crackled with joy. She bounced around the kitchen like employees half her age.

"I've only waited tables at Patterson's." I realized that didn't make me sound very valuable. "But I *could* bake. My mother worked in a bakery for fifteen years and she taught me some things at home."

"Do you have children?"

My eyes filled at the mention of Zach and Haley and I looked down at the floor. "I have two," I said, pretending to cough. "A boy and a girl." I could feel her watching me.

"I had that exact combination, too," she said. She poured a cup of coffee and handed it to me. "You remind me of my grand-daughter. Something in the eyes. I think she's beautiful but I have been accused of being biased. It's completely unfounded. She is stunning. Like you." I looked up at her and smiled. "Has it been one of those days?" I nodded. "I had one of those days once," she said, reaching for a broom hanging on the wall. "It lasted fifteen years and then he decided to run off with the neighbor woman. Two years later she took him for everything he had but I got two kids who have given me four grandchildren so I made out in that deal." She swept the kitchen floor and around Stephanie's feet in small, brisk strokes, sweeping up a small, floury, white pile. I reached for the dustpan hanging on the back wall and knelt in front of her. She took it from me and dumped the pile into the trash can, washing her hands afterward. "Listen, one of my gals is about to go on maternity leave. I thought she should have left last week. When you get to the size of a planet I think you should lay low until the baby comes, but she was determined to work as many days as possible to save up Christmas money. She has three days left, then she'll give birth to little Aaron or Sybil and she'll be off until sometime in January. You interested?"

I had hoped I could find a job that would keep me settled longer, but this was better than nothing. "I am. Is there anyway I could start tomorrow or even today?"

She laughed and handed me a fresh scone. "Try that. We put lemon and cranberries in them during the holidays. It's so good you'll want to smack your mama. I have no idea what that means but my mother always said it so there you go." She watched as I took a bite. It was delicious. She slapped the counter in front of her. "I knew you'd love it." She put her hand on my shoulder and directed me out of the kitchen. "You can start on Tuesday. And we don't do uniforms around here. I just ask that you wear comfortable shoes, keep your breasts covered, and leave room in your pants for air to move through them." I smiled. "I'll provide the apron."

"I really could start today," I said, wondering what I could do to make up for the money I wouldn't be making.

"These things always work themselves out," she said, patting my back. "Your kids will be back in school on Monday, right?" I nodded. "Enjoy them. We'll fill out paperwork when you start. Hold on." She stepped back into the kitchen and moments later appeared holding a white paper sack. "Take this home. It was takeout but nobody came to pick it up."

"Are you sure?"

"Better you take it than us throwing it away."

The smell of the food in the bag reminded me that I hadn't eaten breakfast, and I was anxious to get home. I made my way back through the restaurant and stepped outside into a dazzle of sun and sky. Somehow, the town felt warmer and brighter and I thought maybe it would be a good day after all, but knew it was only a matter of time before the other shoe dropped. I knew it would; it always did.

Patricia Addison picked up the phone and pressed it to her ear. "This is Patricia," she said, scanning a report on her desk.

"I'd like to report a case of child neglect," a man said.

Patricia scribbled notes onto the sheet as the man rambled. She had worked for the Department of Family Services for twenty-one years but for the last four years she'd only worked two days a week so she could stay home with her children. In her experience she often felt she knew when someone was manufacturing a story. She looked over at Roy Braeden who'd been at the department longer than she had but he was on the phone.

"We'll look into it," she said, hanging up. She typed the information into her computer, sighing. She had a feeling she was getting caught up in divorce antics. She sighed louder and Roy waved his arm in the air to shush her, pressing the receiver tighter to his ear.

"Are you trying to blow up a hot air balloon over there?" Roy asked, hanging up the phone. "What's the problem?"

"Nothing. I just have a feeling I'm being sent to this woman's house to scare her. Compliments of her ex."

Roy popped a stick of gum in his mouth and leaned toward her. "That's what that social worker in Florida thought, too. Remember hearing that on the news? He never called on those kids and look what happened."

"Since when haven't I checked out a case?" Patricia said.

"You only work two days a week now. I'm thinking you might be slipping."

"Oh, shut up," she said, turning her back on him.

"Two days a week but it feels like eight," Roy said, opening a file on his desk.

Patricia laughed and labeled a file for this new case. She needed to gather as much information as she could before she visited the home of Angela Christine Eisley.

Marshall stood at the window and watched as people down the street loaded the number four bus at the station. He hated hospitals: the sterile smell, the clickety-clack of the janitor's mop bucket pulled across the floor, the hushed chatter in not so faraway corners, hearts breaking and voices rising as they come to terms with what's happening to their spouse or child or parent in the room beyond the closed door. Marshall pressed closer to the window when he thought he saw the young woman who had been crying on the sidewalk earlier that morning. She was smiling now, waiting in line for the bus. *Another day,* Marshall thought. *Tears, dreaming, weeping, laughing, emergency room visits, the time of day. Nothing stays the same for long.*

He pulled his cell phone out of his pocket and dialed a number, leaning against the window. "Linda? Judy's in the hospital." The doctor stepped into the waiting room and Marshall whispered into the phone, "I'll need to call you right back."

Judy's husband, Dave, stood up when he saw the doctor.

"Mr. Luitweiler?" the doctor asked. The lines between Dave's eyes deepened and his mouth tightened at the sound of his name. "Your wife has had a heart attack," the doctor said. Dave nodded. "We have her stabilized now and are going to move her upstairs to the cardiac cath lab for evaluation."

Dave twisted his ball cap between his hands. "Is she going to be okay?"

"We need to run tests to determine the damage to her heart and arteries and test blood flow. Thankfully, whoever discovered your wife started CPR right away and paramedics began medication therapy as soon as they got her into the ambulance. We're hoping that decreased the amount of heart damage. We'll keep her at least overnight, maybe longer depending on what we find. Once we get her settled you can come be with her."

He left them alone and Dave pushed his thumb and middle finger into his eyes, squeezing them. "Forty years," he said shoving the cap back onto his head. He snapped his fingers. "In the last few minutes they went like that."

"I know," Marshall said, clapping him on the shoulder.

I climbed onto the bus and sat next to the window. I called home to let Mira know that I wouldn't need her for the rest of the day. When I hung up, the phone vibrated and I saw that Brad had left a voice mail. The other shoe was about to drop.

THREE

Judy looked ragged. Her hair sprouted in short, gray tufts on top of her head and she smoothed it down, working her hands through it like pizza dough. Marshall leaned against the windowsill and watched her eat some applesauce. "Linda, Alice, Glenn, your book club, and everyone at work want you to know that they are thinking of you," he said.

"Oh, good grief," she said. "What'd you do? Send up flares in the night?"

"When are you getting out of here?" he asked.

She turned her face toward the open door and yelled, "Not soon enough!"

"She keeps thinking that if she throws enough hints that the doctors will release her sooner," Dave said.

Judy flung the spoon down on the tray. "I want a cream cheese bear claw from Betty's," she said.

"You're not getting a bear claw," Dave said. "So stop asking for one. Bear claws are one of the reasons you're in here." Marshall laughed and leaned against the windowsill. "They're talking stents," Dave said. "Two or three to open blood flow."

"My blood flows," Judy said.

"Not to your heart it doesn't," Dave said.

"Right before Christmas," Judy said, dipping her spoon into the cup of applesauce and turning it over. "This is a terrible time for a stent." She spit the word off her tongue and turned over another spoonful of applesauce.

"What have you been doing to pass the time?" Marshall asked.

"I've been thinking of everything I have to do," she said. "And everything I've done. Of people I love and the people I don't. I keep thinking of things that need to be fixed at home and of things that just need to be left alone."

Marshall whistled through his teeth. "Wow. This downtime has made you so reflective."

She pushed the tray to the side. "No, it hasn't. It's so boring I'm about to lose my mind!" she said, screaming toward the door again. Marshall laughed and stepped away from the bed. "Marsh!" He turned back to her. "I've been thinking about the gal who helped me." He nodded. "If she hadn't been home. I mean . . . if she hadn't been leaving her house . . . can you find her?"

"I can try," he said.

Dave sat on the side of Judy's bed. "Word got to me that the woman left Judy's car at Patterson's. I haven't had time to get it."

"She's a waitress," Judy said. "Her name's Christy, I think."

"I'm on it like warm icing on a gooey cream cheese bear claw," Marshall said, leaving.

"Real nice to do to a sick person," she yelled after him.

The knock came at four thirty Monday afternoon. Zach ran to the door and swung it open before I could warn him *again* about looking to see who it was first. "Hi," he said. I ran around the corner from the kitchen and saw a petite woman with wavy brown hair falling to her shoulders standing on the stairs with some sort of file in her hand. I hated it when salespeople came to the door; I never knew how to get rid of them. I was wearing a tank T-shirt pajama top and ran to the hall closet, grabbing a jacket to wear. I zipped it up and stepped next to Zach.

"Angela Christine Eisley?" the woman

said. My heart stopped. She wasn't a sales-person. Only people in official positions called me by my full name.

"Yes," I said.

She handed me a business card. "My name's Patricia Addison. I'm with the Department of Family Services."

My heart jumped to my throat and I grabbed Zach's arm. "Go back into your room."

"But I'm hungry," he said.

I bent down and whispered in his ear. "Take Haley back into your room right now." He yanked away from me and grabbed his sister's arm, pulling her through the hallway. We weren't off to a good start. I was ordering my hungry children to go to Zach's room. What could she possibly think of me?

The woman looked sympathetic. "I'm sure you know that your ex-husband has called us." Something fluttered high in my chest and I felt nauseous. I couldn't respond. "Mrs. Eisley, I'm only here to talk with you. Can I come in?" I moved aside and was embarrassed by my home. Toys were scattered throughout the living room and papers and bills covered the kitchen table. I gestured toward a chair and she sat down, moving Genevieve out of the way. I took the

75

stuffed dog from her and sat on the edge of the sofa. No one from social services had ever been inside my home. My hands felt numb and I clasped them together.

"You may know some of the allegations your ex-husband is making against you but you may not. It's my job to evaluate those claims. Do you know what he is alleging?" My eyes burned and I shook my head. "He is claiming that you lost your job and a teenager is supervising your children." Something throbbed in my head. How did Brad know I was fired? She read through her notes. "The children are not eating and have been seen outside without socks or shoes." Tears filled my eyes and I covered my face with Genevieve. Her voice was low. "Your ex-husband wants primary custody of the children." Tears spilled over my cheeks and I shook my head back and forth. I couldn't believe what I was hearing. Mrs. Addison reached into her purse and pulled out a small packet of tissues, handing it to me. I took one out and pressed it hard under my eye. She leaned on her knees looking at me. "Just because I'm here doesn't mean that I necessarily believe your husband." I looked up at her and she smiled.

"I did lose my job," I said, finding the words. "But I found another one. I start tomorrow."

"Where will you be working?" she asked, writing something in her notes.

"Betty's Bakery and Restaurant," I said, blowing my nose.

She smiled. "I eat there quite a bit. Do you know your hours yet?"

I felt so stupid. I hadn't even asked Betty what shift I'd be working. "I don't. I go over paperwork on my first day." She nodded and continued to write. "Normally, my kids are in school. I only had a sitter because it was Thanksgiving break. I hate leaving my kids with teenagers but I didn't have a choice."

"Could their father have watched them during that time?" she asked.

I felt trapped. "He's supposed to see them every other weekend."

"Could he have watched them in place of the teenager?"

"I . . ." My voice was trembling. "He hasn't paid me any child support in six months."

Her pen moved quickly over the paper. "Have you taken him to court over child support?"

I squeezed Genevieve in my hands. "Many times. He'll pay it for a while and then stop for months but all the while he's calling here and threatening me with one thing or another." I choked on the words and stopped. "I can't afford to keep taking him into court and he knows that. It's just a game. Why should he see them? He doesn't care about them." I had more to say but I couldn't get the words beyond my throat.

"And the children being seen outside without socks or shoes?"

"They don't even like to play outside when it's cold," I said. An image crossed my mind and I sat forward. "On Saturday, I was helping a woman in the driveway and they did run out for a moment but I told them to get back inside. It was only for a second." In a brief instant I imagined Mrs. Meredith standing at her window and watching. Maybe she was home after all. Maybe Brad came to the house later in the day and she was outside getting her mail and told him all about it. How else would he know?

Patricia jotted more notes on her pad and walked through the hallway. "Can I say hello to the children?"

I jumped up and ran to her side, opening Zach's door. The room was a mess; his bed was unmade and toys and clothes littered the floor. I walked to the bed and pulled up the sheet and blankets, tucking them under the mattress. Patricia stood inside the door and watched them.

Haley noticed her and leaped up, holding Brown Dog. "Do you like dogs?" she asked.

"I love dogs," Patricia said. "I have one real one and about a gazillion stuffed ones."

"What are their names?" Haley asked.

Patricia laughed. "The real one's name is Girl and you'd have to ask my daughters what the stuffed ones are named because I can't keep up with them." I moved around the room and picked up toys, tossing them into the laundry basket we used as a toy box.

"Did you have fun on Thanksgiving break?" Patricia asked.

"No homework," Zach said. "I hate homework."

"I never liked it, either," Patricia said. She sat on the edge of Zach's bed. "How about you, Haley? Do you have homework?"

"Well," Haley said, looking up at her. "My teacher tells us to write our letters all the time and I hate that. Mom makes me sit at the table and write them and I am so bored with that." She grabbed Long Ears and Little Baby and pulled them into her lap. "I do not like writing letters and I do not like math center." She waved her hand in the air. "Way too many blocks to count."

"I never cared for math myself," Patricia

said. "Are you ready for Christmas?"

"I'm always ready for Christmas," Haley said.

"What presents do you want?"

"Star command building set," Zach said. "You can make spaceships and all sorts of docking ports and stuff out of it."

"Wow," Patricia said. "That sounds way over my head. How about you, Haley?"

She didn't have to think. "Wings. So I can fly. I fly all the time at night but I need wings to help me fly during the day."

Patricia smiled. "I bet you'll look just like a princess fairy."

Zach rolled his eyes. "She already *thinks* she's a princess fairy."

Patricia stood and stepped over the toys. "I'll get out of the way so you can keep playing. Bye." The kids waved and I followed her back into the living room. "Thank you, Angela. I know this wasn't comfortable for you."

A wave of urgency rushed to my chest and I was frightened about what she might write in her report. "I love my kids, Mrs. Addison." My heart throbbed and a tear pooled in the corner of my eye as I reached for the doorknob. "I would never do *anything* to hurt them. I don't know what any of this means. I don't know what Brad will do next but you need to know that I will fight him with everything I have for those two kids." I wiped my face and nose with the back of my hand and opened the door.

She stepped outside and turned to me. "I've been doing this for a long time," she said. I wasn't sure how to take that. "I know the difference between mess and filth. I know when kids feel secure and when they feel unloved." She smiled and for the first time since she arrived I took a breath. Her shoes clacked on the sidewalk and she tossed her head around, stopping. "If you're ever in a jam again you should call Glory's Place. It's a place for single moms and kids and people who need help. They'll take good care of your kids."

I pulled the door closed behind me so the kids wouldn't hear. "What's next, Mrs. Addison?"

She put her hand over her eyes to see me in the sun. "I'll file my report." She paused and looked up into the tree that towered over the sidewalk. "And then it's up to your ex-husband."

I sighed. It never ended. "Do I have to let him see them next weekend?"

She pulled sunglasses from her purse and slid them on her face. "No," she said. She paused and I wondered if she was stepping out on a limb, telling me more than she should. "Different states have different rules but due to his negligence in paying child support, I don't think there's a judge in this state that would force you to do that." She threw her hand in the air and I watched as she got into her car and backed down the driveway.

I pushed open the door and moved to the kitchen, assessing the maze of cups and saucers, crayons and coloring books on the countertop. Why couldn't I ever get ahead of anything? Why did it always feel like my life was lived in a cycle of fight, breathe, pick up, put away, fight, breathe, pick up, put away? The morning programs and evening news were filled with pictures and stories of horror and fear, the papers were crammed with worry and dread, homes were fractured, the court dockets were packed with people who hated one another, and the God of my mother seemed powerless to help. Where was the hope in any of that? Where was the help?

I didn't know that it was there, right in the middle of the road, waiting.

Marshall stepped into the office and Jason leaned back in the chair. "I have no idea how Judy navigates through this antiquated software or even *why* she does," he said. He leaned forward and grabbed the mouse, staring at the computer screen. "How is she today?"

"She needs two or three stents," Marshall said, hanging his jacket on the rack. "She'll get them today."

"Before I forget . . . a guy from security came up here looking for you."

Marshall cuffed the sleeve of his denim shirt. "Who in security and what did he want?"

Jason shrugged, reading something on the computer. "I didn't get his name."

"Why not?" Marshall asked, annoyed.

Jason looked up from the screen. "I didn't think —" He stopped.

Marshall waited for him to finish. "What? You didn't think it was import— ?"

"No," Jason said, cutting him off. "I just assumed he'd either —"

"Do you listen when someone speaks or just wait for your turn to talk?"

Jason paused, waiting. "I just assumed he'd come back or call you."

"What's the greeter's name at the front of the store today?"

Jason shrugged, thinking. "I came in the back way today."

Marshall stepped up to his office and

pulled open a file drawer. "I need you to take a quiz," he said. "It's information about the store." He sat at his desk and stapled two sheets of paper together, writing something at the bottom of the second sheet. "If you pass this you'll receive your check for the week." He delivered the test to Jason. "If you don't, I'll keep your check until you do pass it."

Jason took the papers from his grandfather, smiling. "You're kidding, right? I've been running around this store since I was a kid. I'm pretty sure I know everything there is to know."

"You probably do," Marshall said. "But this is something new employees always take and you are a new employee."

Jason put the test in front of him and grabbed a pencil, reading the first question out loud. "When was Wilson's established?" He wrote "1969" and looked up at Marshall. "The fortieth anniversary banner in the front window kind of gives that away." Marshall smiled and stepped up to his office. Jason's pencil flew over the page: *The building was originally a mercantile in the early 1900s, then a law firm, the town library, and a bank in the fifties.* He'd heard his grandparents talk about the building for years. *Marshall and Linda Wilson, store founders.*

Jason thought this was ridiculous. A plaque with the store mission hung on the wall in front of him and he laughed as he copied it onto the paper. Jason turned the paper over for the tenth question: What is the name of our maintenance supervisor? "What?" Jason said, flipping the paper over to look for more questions. "Whatever." He scribbled the name *Ted* down and took the quiz to Marshall.

Marshall put on his reading glasses and scanned the test. "You remembered everything about the building," he said. "That's impressive." He turned the paper over, glanced at the name for the tenth question, and threw the sheets on his desk. "I'll be keeping your check."

"Why? Because of that last question? I know you don't do that for regular employees."

Marshall flipped open a product catalog on his desk. "You're not a regular employee."

Jason laughed. "Why should I know his name?"

"Why shouldn't you?"

"Okay, obviously I would know his name if I was here longer."

Marshall walked to his filing cabinet and stuck the catalog somewhere in the back of it. "Would you? What's the lady's name who lugged your suitcase through the store for you?"

Jason shook his head and laughed. "Denise."

"Wrong," Marshall said. "She has a name. Learn it. Learn who the head of maintenance is." Marshall handed the quiz to Jason. "You can try again in a few days. I'm headed down to security and I need you to pick up Judy's car from Patterson's."

"Why is her car there?" Jason asked, annoyed. First he was taking a ridiculous test and then running errands.

"The woman who gave Judy CPR drove her car there."

"Why?"

Marshall picked up a stack of mail and sifted through it. "Because she had the frame of mind to think that Judy probably wouldn't remember the address of where she was when she had her heart attack. She took the time to be nice!" He ripped up an envelope and threw it away. "Judy said she's a waitress named Christy. Could you please find her and get some contact information? Judy and Dave want to thank her." Marshall looked over his glasses, dangling Dave's keys to Judy's car in front of him. "Did you catch all that?"

Jason's face was vacant. "You mean you want me to go now?"

"Before someone decides to tow her car." Jason grabbed his jacket and opened the door with a huff. Marshall picked up the phone and dialed, pressing the receiver to his ear. "Linda? I think Jason just might drive me crazy."

Before lunch I pulled a sweatshirt over my head and threw on a pair of jeans. I needed to pick up my last check at Patterson's. I held Zach's coat out in front of him.

"I don't want to go," he said.

"Neither do I," I said. "But I need to deposit that check."

"Why?"

He continued to play with his plastic action figures and I lifted his arm and put a sleeve of his coat over it. "If I don't deposit it I'm going to bounce some checks." I shoved the other sleeve over his arm and he flung the coat off in one quick motion. I was too weary to deal with this kind of stuff. "Put it back on, Zach."

"I don't want to go."

I held the coat in front of him again. "Zachary, why do you argue with me every step of the way? Put this coat on and get in the car." He yanked it from me and held it in front of him, determined not to wear it.

"I'm wearing my coat," Haley said, watching us.

I looked up and saw her wearing purple pants shoved down in rain boots, a red princess dress, and a denim jacket with Minnie Mouse embroidered on the front. "Thank you, Haley," I said, pulling Zach's coat from him. "It's too cold to go outside without a coat. Please put it on." He snatched it from me and slipped his arms into it.

All the parking spaces were taken in front of Patterson's so I pulled into one across the street from Wilson's Department Store. Someone was busy outside the fire station hanging a swag of evergreen from one window to the other. An older woman was decorating the three fir trees in the square, hanging enormous bulbs from the branches. I noticed a woman sitting on a bench in the park and thought it was unusual to just *sit* on such a cold day. Maybe she was there to help the woman decorate the trees but she wasn't paying attention to the work being done behind her. It struck me as odd and I sat in my car and watched her, waiting for her to move.

"Can we go look at toys, Mom?" Haley asked when she saw a display of dolls and trains and stuffed animals in Wilson's front window.

I turned the car off, shaking my head. I never shopped at Wilson's. There was never enough time or money. "Not today," I said, opening my car door. "I need to deposit my check."

"How long does that take?" Zach asked. "Can't we look at them for a few minutes?"

It seemed I was always saying no to them. I had no desire to look at toys but said, "Let me pick up my check first."

Jason pulled open the door to Patterson's and stepped into the crowded waiting area. He excused his way through the lunch crowd and waited for the hostess. A young girl with sweat on her upper lip walked breathlessly back to her stand and crossed a name off her list. "I'm looking for Christy," Jason said, leaning his head toward her.

"Is she already here?" the hostess asked, grabbing three menus from their holder on the side of her station. "You can go look for her." She craned her neck and yelled over Jason's head, "Gerald! Party of three!"

"She's not a customer," Jason said. "She's a waitress."

"No, she's not," the hostess said. She looked at the next name and yelled over Jason's head, "Fitz! Party of four!"

"I was told Christy works here," Jason said, emphasizing each word for her. "She drove that gray car right out there," he said, pointing, "and parked it here on Saturday."

The hostess looked behind her and yelled toward a waitress carrying a tray of drinks. "Is there a Christy here?" she asked. The waitress shook her head. "No. Sorry. We have a Lizzy if that helps."

Jason looked at her in disbelief. "No, it doesn't."

I closed the car door and noticed that the woman on the park bench had turned to watch the fir trees being decorated. She was the woman who had stopped me on the street yesterday. She wasn't reading or eating or even talking with anyone. She was just *sitting* there in the cold. I wanted to ask if she'd gone into Patterson's to look for work like I'd suggested but there wasn't time. I took hold of Haley's hand to cross the street. The woman's car I'd driven to work on Saturday was still in the same space I'd left it. *She must still be in the hospital,* I thought. I reached for the restaurant's front door when a young man threw it open.

"Waste of time," he said, barreling into Haley. She lost her balance and landed on my feet.

"Sorry," he said, without looking or stopping to help Haley.

"He's fast," Haley said, taking my hand.

"He's rude," I said, ushering her through the door.

The waiting area was full as several people crowded the new hostess. I had heard she was going to be starting today. We had gone through a lot of hostesses during my time at Patterson's. She was flustered and seated two tables in a row in Jean's section instead of staggering the seating. Rod probably put her up front with very little training; that was usual protocol for him. Renee saw me and threw her index finger in the air before disappearing to the back. I pulled Zach and Haley off to the side and waited. Renee turned the corner, smiling at me. "Rod's not here," she said.

"Lucky me," I said, taking the check from her.

She reached into her pocket and pulled out a bill. "Here," she said. "From your table on Saturday."

The hostess led a party of three past us. "I didn't even take their order," I said, shoving the check in my purse. "Why would they leave me a tip?"

She smiled. "They just did. That's all."

I looked at the money. "Twenty dollars!" Renee's eyes were wide. No one ever left a tip bigger than a five-dollar bill at Patterson's and even that was rare. "I'm not taking that, Renee."

Renee shoved the money in my purse. "You are taking this money," she said. "Now stop making a scene."

She tried to make a quick getaway but I grabbed her arm, pulling the bill from my purse. "No! I am not taking this. It's yours!"

"I'll take it," Zach said, holding out his hand.

I looked at Renee and sighed. "Why would you do this?"

She hugged me around the neck. "I'm just passing it on," she said, disappearing around the corner.

The hostess gave an awkward smile and I moved the kids through the front door. A car pulled into an empty space in front of the restaurant. "It was just here," I said to myself.

"What was just here?" Haley asked.

"There was a car right here a minute ago," I said, looking up and down the street. "But now it's gone." Haley tugged me toward Wilson's and Zach ran ahead. As I walked I watched vehicles on the other side of the square and tried to spot the woman's car.

Haley pulled me harder and I gave up, opening the door to Wilson's. Large green and red and silver ornaments hung from the ceiling along with an angel sitting in a snowflake and elves holding brightly wrapped packages. A large Christmas tree sprung up from the center of the cosmetics counter covered with gold angels and strands of fake pearls.

The toy department was on the bottom floor. We took the stairs down and the banister was wrapped like a candy cane. Santa's workshop sat in the middle of the floor. "Oh, great," I muttered.

"Whoa!" Haley said, jumping off the bottom step. She ran to the gingerbread fence and read the hours on the giant lollipop. "What's this say?" she said, waving at me.

"He's not here right now," I said, reading the hours Santa was on duty. I noticed he was due in twenty minutes. I didn't want to hear Zach and Haley tell Santa everything they wanted for Christmas, knowing there was no way I could possibly buy half of it. The kids ran through the aisles and Zach picked up a magnetic interlocking building toy and Haley held a Barbie doll in each hand.

"Can I get this, Mom?" Zach asked, holding the box in his hands.

"Not right now," I said. "Make out a Christmas list when you get home and we'll see."

Zach put the box back on the shelf. "That means never," he said.

"Maybe Santa will bring it," Haley said.

"There isn't any Santa," he said, pushing past her. I flashed him a look to keep his mouth closed. I wasn't sure if Zach no longer believed in Santa or if he was merely convincing himself he didn't exist because he didn't want to face the disappointment.

"There is so," Haley said, following him. I pulled a doll off the shelf that sang when you pushed her necklace and I tried to distract Haley with it.

I picked up a box that contained a small piano for a doll and turned it over, glancing at the price: fifty-nine dollars. *For one toy!* I thought. I wandered through the aisles and checked the price on a small princess castle for dolls. Thirty-five dollars. A large package of pretend food was twenty dollars. I knew I needed to work extra hours at Betty's through Christmas to help pay for gifts. I lifted a heart-shaped box from the shelf that children were supposed to paint and decorate themselves. The thought of leading Haley through a time-consuming craft made my head hurt and I felt guilty for never having enough time or patience. I was reading the instructions on the back of the box when the saleslady's voice at the cash register on the other side of the toy racks caught my attention. Her tone was low but insistent as she spoke with someone and I leaned closer to the aisle to hear what they were arguing about.

"I heard you say 'Merry Christmas,' " a young man's voice said.

"No, I told her to have a great Christmas," the saleswoman said. I bent low so I could see her through the games stacked in front of me. She was a black woman in her mid-forties wearing a bright red sweater and green sparkly scarf around her neck.

"Same thing," the man said. "Nobody says 'Merry Christmas' anymore. Just say 'Happy Holidays' and be done with it."

The woman was quiet. "Is this a new policy or something?" she finally asked, flipping the end of the scarf over her shoulder.

"No, it's just something you need to do."

"Who says? Your grandfather?" She didn't give him a chance to answer. "Because this does not sound like Marshall. This doesn't make any sense. We don't sell holiday trees; we sell Christmas trees. We don't sell holiday gifts; we sell Christmas gifts." She was on a roll and her voice tightened. "We don't eat *holiday* dinner; we eat Christmas dinner. People don't put out manger scenes because the holiday child was born. It's not *just* a holiday that brings people into this store every year at this time. It's Christmas. No one looks at their calendar in December and says, 'Oh, holiday is coming up on the twenty-fifth. They say Christmas. So 'Merry Christmas' is what I will say."

"Suit yourself," the guy said. I heard his footsteps on the stairs and I peered around the toys to see the saleswoman. She was mumbling and fanning herself.

"There is no Christy," Jason said, entering the office.

Marshall stepped down from his office. "No Christy right now or no Christy period?"

Jason sat down and moved the mouse around to awaken the computer. "Period."

"Did you ask if anyone had heard of her?" Jason shook his head. "Maybe she works at Lemon's or Betty's. You should have tried those other restaurants."

Jason rolled a pencil between his thumb and fingers. "Why? We *have* the car."

Marshall felt something rise in his chest. "The car is not the point," he said, throwing stale donuts away one at a time into the trash can. "Have you thought of anyone's circumstances besides your own in the last year?" Jason didn't say anything. "Has anyone's situation brought tears to your eyes or made you think differently about life?"

"I guess," Jason said, shrugging.

"If you're not sure then you probably haven't. Here's the deal. This woman saved Judy's life and Judy wants to thank her, whoever she is, wherever she works. It shouldn't be that hard." He threw the empty box into the can with a thud and walked out into the store.

"She doesn't work there," Jason said to the closed door. "How am I supposed to know where she is?"

I walked up the stairs with Zach and Haley following.

"Did you find everything you were looking for?" An older man asked me on the top step.

"Marshall! I need to talk to you." The saleswoman from the toy department was bounding up the stairs behind me, her hands flapping around a cloud of black hair. Regardless of where that man was headed he was now stuck with a woman set loose. I never had the opportunity to answer him but truth was I didn't find anything that I was looking for but had long stopped expecting to discover it.

I wanted to find something to fill the emptiness, something that would drive back the dark and ease my fear. I wanted to find something that would fight for me the way the saleswoman fought for Christmas. I wanted to find that kind of fierce hope. I took hold of Zach's and Haley's hands and walked to the car. Like my mother always said, sometimes you don't get everything you want. Even at Christmas.

FOUR

Jason pulled his coat tight around him and ran across the back parking lot toward the service entrance. Two men were busy at work unloading a shipment and Jason kept his head down as he took the stairs in quick steps, avoiding any conversation with the men as he opened the door. He stopped and turned his head watching them; small puffs filled the air as they talked. One man pulled his winter cap further down on his head, banging his hands together. "Hey," Jason yelled. The man turned to look at him. "Good morning!" Both men stopped and waited for Jason to say something. "Um. . . . I don't know you guys. I'm Jason. I'm helping in the office while Judy's out."

"Bill," the older guy said. "And Hutch," he said, pointing to the other man inside the back of the truck.

Jason shoved his hands into his pockets. "And you work in shipping?"

"And merchandise," Bill said, pulling his cap tighter to his head.

Jason repeated their names to himself as he walked through the back door and to the security office. "Bill and Hutch, Hutch and Bill," he whispered, pushing open the door. A man in his thirties or so spun in his seat at the sound of the door. "Hi," Jason said. "I'm working upstairs while Judy's out. I didn't catch your name yesterday when you came into the office."

"Kevin," the security guard said, spinning his wedding band on top of the desk.

"Great!" Jason said. "Do you know the head of maintenance?"

"You mean Larry?" Kevin said.

"Right! Larry. Sorry to interrupt you." Jason closed the door and walked through the back hallway. "Phil, Hutch, Kevin, and Larry. Hutch, Kevin, Phil, and Larry." He stuck his head around the corner to see the toy department and was determined to learn the names of the employees there. He saw the black woman from the day before and decided he'd do that another day. He took the stairs by two and stopped at the main floor. Two women were behind the cosmetics and jewelry counter. "Hi," he said, putting his hands in his jeans pockets. "I'm Jason and I'm helping out while Judy's gone. I don't know either of you."

"I'm Laura," the woman in cosmetics said. "That's Renata."

Jason nodded and added their names to his list: "Phil, Hutch, Kevin, Larry. Laura and Renata," he said, pulling the door open to the office. He searched Judy's desk for a sticky note or scrap sheet of paper he could write the names on but didn't find anything. The cabinet across the room held several office supplies but no paper or notepads. Jason stepped up into Marshall's office and pulled open the top drawer of the desk, sitting when he discovered a small jewelry box at the back shoved behind a package of staples. A simple gold necklace with a small diamond hanging from it glittered against the black velvet box.

"Caught ya!" Marshall said, causing Jason to jump.

"You got a woman on the side I don't know about?" Jason asked, dangling the necklace from his fingers.

Marshall hung his coat on the rack and laughed. "Anniversary gift."

Jason put the necklace into the box and stuffed it to the back of the drawer again. "This is your safe?"

Marshall shrugged. "Safe enough."

"How long has it been in here?"

Marshall shooed him away from his desk. "I don't remember when I bought it."

"Why'd you buy a diamond for Nana? Nana of the 'just make me something with your own hands or wash the dishes for me and that's all I want for Christmas'?"

Marshall laughed, pulling out the necklace again, looking at it. "Haven't you ever seen anything that leaves you breathless and humbled at the same time?"

Jason looked at the necklace. Besides the diamond it was plain in every way. "You mean that?"

Marshall shook his head. "Your nana." He lay the necklace back into the box and closed the lid. "What were you looking for anyway?"

"There's no paper anywhere in this office," Jason said.

Marshall walked to the kitchenette area for a pot of coffee but no one had made it yet. "Judy was headed out for supplies when she ended up in the hospital." He waved the empty coffeepot in the air. "See, I'm no good without her. She remembers all this stuff." He pointed to the phone. "Call Derek at the Office House and ask him what Judy normally buys and then go pick it up."

"Can I take that test again first?" Jason knew if he didn't take the test soon the names would leave him.

"Brew up a pot of coffee and I'll give it to you."

The kitchenette area was around the corner from the copier and included a small sink, a coffeemaker, and a tin full of Marshall's favorite cookies from Betty's Bakery. Jason rinsed out the coffee carafe and put in a fresh filter, filling it with ten scoops of ground Columbian supreme. "Hutch, Phil, Kevin, and Larry. No. *Bill,* Hutch, Kevin, and Larry," he said, flipping on the coffeemaker.

He sat at the desk and Marshall handed him the quiz. Jason's pencil flew over the first nine questions and stopped at number ten. The original question had been crossed out and Marshall's handwriting was above it: How is Judy doing today?

Jason sighed. He should have known Marshall would mess with the questions. He scribbled on the line next to the question: *Much better and improving.* Flipping to the next page the last question read, "What is the name of the woman in the toy department?" Jason shook his head and wrote *Mrs. Claus.*

"Round two completed," Jason said, laying the test on Marshall's desk.

Marshall put his glasses on and scanned

the answers. "Nice spin on Judy's condition." Jason smiled. "How is she really?" Marshall asked, looking over his glasses.

Jason raised his eyebrows, resigned. "I don't know. I should but I don't."

"She's being released sometime this morning. The doctor put two stents in her heart yesterday."

"Oh," Jason said. He knew his grandfather was trying to make him feel bad for not knowing that. "I thought you were going to ask me the maintenance supervisor's name."

"Do you know his name?" Marshall asked, leaning back in his chair.

"Yes. And I know the two guys out in shipping and merchandise. Phil and Hutch."

"Close," Marshall said. He stood and walked down the steps from his office to the coffeemaker. "Now what's the woman's name in toys?"

Jason groaned and put his face in his hands. "I have no idea."

"Well, you offended her. It's always a good rule of thumb to know the name of the person you're offending."

Jason shook his head. His grandfather was getting on his nerves. "I don't understand the point here. I know you want me to know people's names but —"

"Wrong." Marshall said, taking a bite of a

chocolate chip cookie. "I don't want you to know their names. I want you to know *them*."

Jason moved past Marshall and filled a cup with black coffee. "Okay. I'll take the test again and know *everyone's* name."

Marshall pushed the last bite of cookie into his mouth and stepped toward his office. Jason hadn't understood a word he said; he knew that. "I need you to work on finding Christy today," he said, closing his office door.

Jason growled, grabbing his coat. He figured he should find Christy as soon as possible so Marshall would leave him alone and he could get on with his life. He pulled up the zipper and opened the door leading into the store. "*Bill* and Hutch!" he yelled toward Marshall's office. Marshall laughed as the door slammed shut.

Thankfully, Zach and Haley got on the school bus as I got in the car for my first day at work. Their final day of school was on the eighteenth and I was already stressed about finding a sitter for the two-week Christmas break. Although she had failed me more than once, I called and left a message for Allie to see if she could watch them anytime during the break. I left a message for Mira as well, thinking that maybe I could piecemeal together a group of sitters. I hung up the phone as I pulled into the parking lot behind Betty's.

The computerized ordering system was different from Patterson's and I felt dull and inadequate as I made one mistake after another, running to the kitchen to correct my botched orders. "It just takes a few times," Karen said, showing me again how to void an order. She was a petite yet stout woman with short-cropped raven black hair and a small sparkly nose stud. On warmer days her husband drove her to work on the back of his Harley-Davidson. Cliff had a surly beard, a gut out to here, and a laugh that could dismantle a truck engine. He liked to pat her butt as she climbed off the back of his bike and she'd plant a kiss on lips lost somewhere in the middle of his whiskers. "When your order's up the guys in the back will yell your name," Karen said. I looked at her: I was used to scrambling to a kitchen to check on orders. "Betty started that years ago when it was just her and a couple of employees. It's actually a lot better than running back to the kitchen every couple of minutes. It's become part of the vibe here over the years."

Karen helped me input an order for a

family of four. A husband and wife sat at a table with their two small children and I watched the father play tic-tac-toe on a napkin with his young son. Every time I saw a family like that my heart hurt. "We still need milk for her," the woman said, pointing to her toddler daughter.

"I forgot. I'm sorry," I said, rushing to the waitress station. I filled a Styrofoam cup and put a lid on it. "There you go," I said, setting it down in front of the girl. "Sorry," I said to her parents.

"We come in here once a week," the mother said. "So we know you're new." She cut her daughter's French toast. "You won't remember our names yet but I'm Julie. This is Clayton and these two belong to us: Ava and Adam." She looked up at me and smiled. "Don't let the jerks get you down."

A man at a table with six other men lifted his coffee cup and I headed toward them. "Those are the mechanics from City Auto Service," Karen said, handing me a fresh pot of coffee. "Jack Andrews and that crew have been coming in here for years so you'll see them a lot." I filled their cups and carried away the empty plates.

I noticed two older women sitting at a booth and jumped, not knowing how long they had been sitting there. I grabbed two ice waters and smiled as I approached them. They were opening a stack of mail sitting on the table. "Good morning," I said, setting the waters in front of them.

"Well, who are you?" the first woman said. She was wearing a red sweatshirt with a mouse dressed like an elf on the front of it. "I know everyone in here but I don't know you. Where's your name tag?"

"As you can see, Gloria excels in proper etiquette," the second woman said. "She should write the manners column for the newspaper."

The first woman laughed and tiny, loose salt-and-pepper curls bounced around her face. "I'm Gloria Bailey," she said, picking up a strand of curls and pinning them on top of her head.

"I'm Miriam," the second woman said in an accent I couldn't pinpoint yet. Her hair hung in a sleek, honey-colored bob and a large diamond ring sparkled on her right hand.

"I'm Christine. I don't have a name tag yet."

"Are you from here, Christine?" Gloria asked.

"Please, Gloria, must you put this poor woman through your twenty questions? Let her learn her job without being subjected to you so early in the morning."

"I am taking the time to know her," Gloria said. "You could learn to do the same."

"I know all the people I want and most of them I don't like."

"Miriam looks good on the outside," Gloria said, "but inside she's nothing but tacky."

I wasn't sure if they were angry at each other or if this was normal banter between the two of them. "Where are you from?" I asked.

They answered Georgia and England in unison.

Gloria looked up at me. "I would like bacon, egg, and cheese on an onion bagel with a cup of coffee. Miriam here will have a boiled egg, medium yolk, a piece of dry wheat toast, and a cup of English breakfast tea. I'd like to say that we vary from time to time but I'm afraid we're old and set in our ways and this is what we order all the time."

I hurried to the computer so I could input their orders. It seemed like I was taking too long and I sensed someone standing behind me. Tasha was in college and I felt she was assured that she was far more brilliant than me and I'm sure she was. "I don't think I've done this right," I said, looking at her.

She glanced at the screen. "Bacon, egg,

and cheese on an onion bagel and a boiled egg, medium yolk, with dry wheat toast. Just send it through. If you take this long for each order you'll never get to all your tables. You have a guy at number six."

I looked up and noticed the young man. He was tapping the corner of the menu on the table. He looked up as I approached and smiled. He had sandy brown hair, dark eyes, and solid, square shoulders.

"Hi," he said, laying his menu on the table.

He held my gaze and I felt self-conscious. I had thrown my hair into a quick ponytail and forgotten to put on eye shadow. "Do you know what you'd like or do you need a few minutes?"

"If I need a few minutes that means you'll get to come back to my table again, right?"

Was I blushing? "Right," I said.

"Then, yes, I will definitely need a few minutes." *Was he flirting with me? No, couldn't be. He's younger than I am. He must have a girlfriend.* I turned to go but he stopped me. "What do you recommend?"

Why would that question make me smile? *Get over yourself, Christine.* "People really like the bacon, egg, and cheese on a bagel."

"Do you like it?" he asked. His smile turned up into a dimple on one side of his face.

"I love bagel sandwiches, sure." I sounded so stupid. Actually, I didn't care for bagel sandwiches one way or the other. I walked toward the kitchen to check on my orders. What just happened back there? Did that guy flirt with me? *No, he didn't. He didn't,* I told myself. My track record with men had been rocky to say the least. I had a knack for attracting losers. Since Brad left I had dated two men who turned out to be more messed up and dysfunctional than me. I shook my head. There's no way the guy at table six thought anything of me. *I look terrible. And even if he did flirt, he'd stop flirting the second he heard I have two children.* I put the food on a tray and placed a sprig of parsley and an orange slice on each plate before picking up a glass of water at the waitress station along with a coffeepot.

When I turned the corner I could feel the guy at table six watching me as I walked to Gloria and Miriam's table. "In case you're wondering," Gloria whispered, "yes, he's still looking."

"He's too young," I said, putting her bagel sandwich in front of her.

"For you maybe," she said. "He's fair game for me and Miriam." Miriam laughed out loud.

"Shh," I said. "He's going to know we're

111

talking about him."

"Let's use some sort of code," Gloria said, watching as I poured her coffee. "Let's just refer to him as TS for table six. Get it?" Miriam rolled her eyes.

I filled the cups of the mechanics behind me one last time and left the bill on the table. When I turned around TS was smiling, his arm slung over the back of the bench. "Are you ready to order?" I asked, pushing loose hair behind my ear.

"Not really, but as much as I'd like it I don't think your boss would let you keep coming to my table empty-handed." My face felt as red as Gloria's sweatshirt. He *was* flirting with me. Somehow this guy thought I was pretty and I felt like a high schooler again. He smiled and my stomach flipped. "I'll have the bagel sandwich you recommended. On what kind of bagel?"

"Onion," I said, writing. "With a cup of coffee."

I walked away and hoped he wasn't looking at my butt but hoped he *was* looking at my butt. Gloria and Miriam nodded; he was. I turned the corner to the waitress station and stepped next to Karen. "Do you know the guy at table six?" I asked. She turned to see him. "Don't look at him!" I said between my teeth. "He's looking over here."

Karen opened a bakery case and pretended to move some pastries around, looking at him through the glass window. "I have no idea," she said. She closed the case and stood back up. "I've never seen him before. Gloria and Miriam would know him. They know everybody."

I finished inputting his order into the computer. "Not *everybody*," I said.

Karen poured sugar packets from a bag into a bin beside the coffeemakers. "He's still looking over here."

"He'll stop looking when he learns I have two kids."

"You never know," she said.

I put a cup on my tray and then picked up the coffeepot and a small pitcher of cream. Was Karen right? Could he be the kind of guy who would be interested in a woman with children? *No way,* I said to myself. Several customers motioned for me to warm up their coffee as I passed and I could see TS watching me.

I walked to his table, set the empty cup in front of him, and filled it with coffee, setting the cream beside it. "Just black," he said. I put the cream back on my tray and turned to walk away. "Hey," TS said. I stopped to look at him. He really was gorgeous. "Do you know Christy?" My heart stopped beating. Only Brad called me that. My head started spinning. Brad must have sent him here to find out what kind of hours I was working or anything else he could dig up and use against me. I was going to be slapped with another court appearance or he was going to call my home when he knew I was working a late shift and leave countless intimidating voice mails. I rushed to the kitchen and tried to catch my breath. How could I be so stupid? This guy wasn't interested in me.

"Are you all right?" Karen asked, balancing a tray of food on her hip.

"Yeah, I'm good," I said. "But could you finish taking care of table six? I think my ex-husband sent him here to look for me. He's looking for Christy. Only my ex calls me that. He doesn't know who I am. Please don't tell him, Karen."

"Has he been rude or something?" I shook my head. "Then what makes you think your ex-husband sent him here? What would be the point?"

I was taken off guard and annoyed. "The point would be to get at me any way he could. That's what he does."

Karen could sense that I was frustrated.

"I'll finish the table. Don't worry about it."

I walked to the computer and closed out the rest of my tables. My face was hot and my heart pounded in my ears. I felt so foolish and embarrassed. For a moment I had felt pretty again and my mind had wandered off in thoughts of romance and adult conversation instead of the familiar anxieties, frustrations, and disappointments. I never should have allowed myself to feel that way. Stupid, stupid. I slipped Gloria and Miriam's bill onto Karen's tray because their table was much too close to TS. "Thanks, Karen."

"No problem. But you know, that kid doesn't seem like the hurtful type. I think he's full of himself, not nearly as good-looking as he thinks he is, and I know my husband could take him out but I don't think it's in his makeup to be intimidating."

I could see TS looking around for me and Gloria and Miriam caught more than an earful from Karen as she finished out their table. For once in my life I was thankful I didn't have a section full of customers waiting for me but instead I was waiting for them to finish. I busied myself cutting up more orange slices in the kitchen, waited for TS to leave, and hoped I'd never see him again.

■ ■ ■ ■

Jason shoved his hands in his coat pocket and headed back to Wilson's through the town square. He walked to the gazebo and thought of playing with his sister inside it as his parents and grandparents sat on a nearby park bench and talked. He was always the superhero saving his sister from the cruel villain, Dakmar the Dark. He thought the name was so stupid; his sister made it up. He looked at the buildings surrounding the square: the firehouse that had recently been painted a brighter shade of red, the attorney's office with the giant wreaths hanging in the windows, the library where he and his sister would sit for story time every morning they visited, and the drugstore where his grandparents would take them for candy and ice cream (all in secret so his mother wouldn't know how much junk they were eating). He smiled at the memories.

He thought of squirrels running up the elm trees and people playing with their children and dogs. He remembered the shopkeepers who spied his grandparents in the park and joined them for a cracker with cheese out of the family picnic basket. He thought how some of them had labored hard over the decades and how some didn't work hard enough so their storefront signs and names were now long forgotten. He recalled conversations of business lost and some gained, of customers who moved, gave birth, or died, and how at the end of the crackers and cheese he would take his grandfather's hand and walk back to Wilson's with him.

Jason's cell phone rang and he saw it was Ashley. He let it ring in his hand, wondering if he should answer it. He thought of the town square and of cheese and crackers and the waitress' pretty face at Betty's and put the phone back in his pocket.

When he got back to the store a familiar voice greeted him. "Good morning, Jason," she said.

He racked his brain for her name but came up empty. "Good morning," he said, walking past her. He thought of the ridiculous quiz Marshall was making him take and stopped. "I don't think I remember your name."

"Debbie," she said.

He nodded, remembering now. He looked at a young girl changing mannequins in the front window. "And who's that?"

"Lauren," she said.

"Got it," he said, committing the names to memory. He walked into the office and hung his jacket on the coatrack. "I went to all the downtown restaurants and there isn't a Christy."

Marshall pursed his lips, scratching his forehead. "Maybe Judy got her name wrong. She wasn't exactly in the best frame of mind. Well, we can't say we haven't tried." He looked at Jason. "Did you remember to bring back another sack of cookies?"

"You didn't tell me to bring back cookies."

"Sure I did."

"No, you didn't. And you don't need cookies anyway. You'll end up like Judy."

"You sound just like your grandmother," Marshall said.

Jason sat in Judy's chair and talked loud enough for Marshall to hear him. "The lady who helped with my suitcase is named Debbie, by the way," he said. "Can I get my check now?"

"Only when you answer all the questions correctly as you *take* the test, not after the fact." Marshall stepped out of his office and stood in front of Jason. "How would you like to volunteer at Glory's Place?"

"What in the world is Glory's Place?"

"It's a place where underprivileged parents can learn skills or leave their children while they work. They're always short-handed over there and I got a call this morning from Gloria Bailey who asked if I knew anyone who could help. It'd be great exposure for you if you did some hands-on work."

"In what way?" Jason asked, swiveling in the chair.

Marshall picked up a stack of mail on the edge of Judy's desk and tapped it in his palm. "You'll meet people who need help." He slapped the mail in his hand and walked up to his office. "If you could head over there this week that'd be great. I told Gloria she could expect you." The warmth of the gazebo left Jason. If he wanted to volunteer somewhere it would be a place of his choosing, not something his grandfather dictated. "And the next time you're in Betty's bring back a sack of cookies."

Jason put his hands on top of his head and leaned back in the chair. "You don't need cookies."

"Tomorrow will be fine!" Marshall said, yelling from his office.

The breakfast rush ended around nine thirty. I scrambled to get my tables ready for the lunch crowd, refilling the sugar and napkin dispensers, and setting a ketchup and mustard bottle on each table. I noticed a woman sit down at the table closest to the window and walked to the waitress station. "She won't eat anything," Karen said. "She just orders a day-old pastry and a cup of coffee. She's weird. Never talks much and never leaves a tip."

I filled a glass with ice and water and picked up a menu, taking them to the woman's table. I set the water down and recognized her as the woman I had told to apply for the waitress job at Patterson's. "Hi," I said. She didn't look at me but I noticed she wasn't wearing makeup, her arms were thin, blue veins ridged the top of her hands, and her shoulder blades looked like bony wings down her back. "Did you get the job at Patterson's?" She looked up at me, confused. "I told you they needed a waitress."

A glimmer of recognition flashed in her eyes. "I went in there and talked to a lady about it but I didn't fill out an application. I've never been a waitress before. I wouldn't be very good at it."

"You'd be great at it. If I can do it anybody can do it. I'm Christine by the way." She didn't tell me her name. The shirt she wore accentuated her long, thin arms. "Didn't you wear a coat today?" I asked. She shook her head. "You must be freezing. You're like my kids. They run out the door and I have to chase them down to put a coat on them." I put the menu in front of her and she pushed it away.

"Day-old pastry and a cup of coffee," she said.

I picked up the menu. "What kind of — ?"

"Doesn't matter," she said, cutting me off.

I brought her a chocolate chip and nut pastry because it looked the freshest and set a cup of coffee in front of her then went back to cleaning and prepping the tables in my section. I didn't see her leave. She left two dollars on the table. "No tip," I said, putting the money into the cash register.

"Told ya," Karen said.

I closed out my last table at three forty. On my first day I'd met many of the regulars — the old man whose teeth didn't fit and clicked when he ordered, Adrian who was painted and pierced like a carnival attraction, the fat lady with hair the color of a ripe mango, Monica with her fraternal twins who fight like enemies, the mechanics from City Auto Service, Gloria and Miriam, the Asian college students who met for coffee after their English as a second language class, the single mom and her terror toddler "Lovey Love" with his big, diapered butt, and the tall, angular woman who rolls her big, dark eyes when she talks and laughs from her gut. They were an odd collection but I liked them all.

I glanced at the clock on the wall. The kids would be getting home in ten minutes. I hated it that they'd be there by themselves for a few minutes before I got home and hoped that Brad would never find out. "How was your first day?" I turned to see Betty calling me from the kitchen where she was rolling out dough.

"It was great. I loved it," I said, trying my best to sound excited.

She leaned her head to the side. "Take that sack of cookies home to the kiddos. They're not even day-old anymore. They're two days old. But kids won't notice." I grabbed the cookies and realized I was starving. I hadn't eaten since breakfast. "Take that, too," Betty said, cocking her head to the other side. "That was a to-go order no one ever picked up." That didn't sound right. Another takeout order that wasn't picked up? "We'll just throw it away if you don't take it," she said, placing the dough in a pie plate.

I threw on my coat and ran to the car,

opening the sack as the engine warmed. It was a turkey, swiss, and bacon sandwich on rye. I took a bite and sighed. Wow, was it good!

Zach held his arm over Haley's chest, keeping her in the seat until the bus stopped. "Remember," he said, "as soon as the door opens run as fast as you can to the front door."

"What if she sees us?" Haley asked, holding her pink backpack in her lap.

"It's okay if she sees us," Zach says. "Just don't make eye contact with her. No one can look the Bat Lady in the eye and live." He shoved her backpack in front of her face. "Here. Hold this up so you can be safe." The bus stopped and he jumped up. "Come on. Run for your life." Haley held the backpack in front of her eyes and bolted for the stairs.

Haley staggered up the driveway and stumbled on the stairs. "I can't see," she said.

Zach stopped when he saw Mrs. Meredith standing at her door watching them. "Quick," he said to Haley, rushing for the front door. "The Bat Lady's watching us. Get the key and run in the house." Haley fumbled for the key under the flowerpot and dropped it into the flower bed. Zach threw his backpack onto the porch and pushed her out of the way, lying on his stomach to retrieve the key. "The Bat Lady could have eaten us by now," he said. He put the key into the lock and they fell into the house, breathing heavy.

The door was unlocked when I got home at four twenty and I stepped inside, yelling for Zach and Haley. "Just a second!" Zach yelled from his room.

"No," I said, hanging up my coat. "Come now." They ran down the hall and I walked to the kitchen to start dinner for them. "When you come home from school you *must* lock the door behind you."

"I forgot," Zach said. "We were running from the Bat Lady and we ran right into our bedrooms."

I wanted to laugh. "You can't forget," I said. "You've been home for thirty minutes and a lot can happen in thirty minutes. You have to remind each other to lock the door. Even when Mrs. Meredith is watching."

Zach looked upset. I know it felt like I was always yelling at them. I lifted the sack of cookies. "Look," I said, reminding myself of my own mother coming home from the bakery. "Cookies. I'll even let you eat one

124

before dinner." Haley rushed for the bag and I pulled it open, watching her reach inside.

"Chocolate chip!" she said, screeching.

I held the bag in front of Zach but he didn't move. I reached in and handed a cookie to him. "I'm not mad," I said in his ear. "I just want you and Haley to be safe."

He took the cookie and shoved half of it in his mouth. "Can we put up the tree tonight?"

I opened a cabinet and pulled out a pot. "Not tonight, Zach. I'm too tired to make that mess."

"You're always too tired," he said, shoving the rest of the cookie in his mouth. "That's why I brought it in. Look!" He pointed to a corner of the living room where he had dragged our tiny four-foot tree from the deck shed. I sighed. "Mom, everyone has Christmas lights up. Even the Bat Lady has a tree in her front window. Can we decorate it?"

I was defeated. He opened his mouth to say more but I cut him off. "Try doing some homework while I make dinner and then you can decorate some of it." He dashed down the hallway and I walked to the end table by the sofa to make room for the tree.

"Mom, do you think Santa will bring me

fairy wings so I can fly?" Haley asked.

She was stalling. "I don't know, babe. You need to start your homework."

"I hate homework," she said, blowing out crumbs as she talked.

"All you have to do is practice writing a letter," I said. "What is it today? *S*?"

She folded her arms. "No. It's *r* and I hate *r*. It's too hard and nothing good starts with *r*."

I cleared the lamp and a picture from the table and set them on the floor. "Lots of good things start with *r*. Rain."

"I don't like rain," she said, finishing the cookie. "It gets me wet."

I spread the tablecloth over the end table and set the tree on top of it. It was a sad and pitiful little thing. "How about rabbit?"

"I like rabbits," she said, tearing open the bag of cookies.

I took the bag from her and put it on the sofa. "Then think of rabbits as you practice your *r*'s." She started to whine as I pulled and plumped each branch on the tree. "Don't start whining, Haley. It never gets you anywhere. Go practice your *r*'s. You could have had them done by now." Her shoulders deflated and she huffed away.

"Mom!" Zach yelled from his room. "I need help with this."

I sighed. Each evening was the same as I was torn in a dozen directions at once — dinner, cleaning, homework, laundry, bills, and tonight, decorating the Christmas tree. I heard my name at least fifty times a night. I pulled a jar of spaghetti sauce from a cabinet and opened it. "Can it wait until after dinner?"

"You told me to do homework now."

"Hold on," I said, pouring the sauce into a pan. I began to fill another pan with water when someone knocked on the door. I turned the water off and walked out of the kitchen. I could see through the window at the top of the door that it was my landlord. I was late with December's rent.

"Hi, Ed," I said, opening the door. "I'm sorry I'm late with my check. I can get rent to you by the end of the week."

His face was blank and I knew something was wrong. "Christine, I'm sorry," he said. I felt my heart sink and knew what was coming. "I've always been willing to work with you but you've only paid partial payments for the last four months."

I stepped outside so the kids couldn't hear. "I know but I always catch up. You know I do."

He looked down at the sidewalk and pushed a pinecone out of the way with his foot. "At first you did and I worked with you as best I could. I've raised the rent on the other units eight months ago but kept yours the same. I know it's tough to pay bills on your own but I have to pay the mortgage on these units and I just don't see how you can catch up now." He handed me a letter. "I'll need you to be out by the end of January." I couldn't find enough air in my lungs to push out a word. "I'm sorry."

I watched him drive away and my legs felt heavy on the stairs. I had no idea how to pick them up and walk back into the house. For a fleeting moment I thought of calling my mother but let the thought pass. She wasn't in the position to dole out that kind of money and deep down I was too embarrassed to ask for help. The phone rang on the other side of the door and I pushed it open. My thighs felt like Jell-O as I crossed to the kitchen and saw on caller ID that it was Brad. I hated him and his phone calls and his young friend he sent into the restaurant today. I despised the constant struggle and worries and inability to get ahead. Zach called me from his room and I pushed a dish towel to my mouth, listening as the phone continued to ring.

After the blow from Ed I lacked the physical and mental energy to do much with the tree so I relegated myself to untangling lights and putting hooks on the ornaments. I didn't stop Zach when he put too many lights on the tree so it looked like a small explosion in our window or Haley when she put cotton balls on each branch to look like snow, and I didn't say a word as most of those white, puffy balls ended up on the table. As soon as the last snowman was hung on a branch I made the kids brush their teeth and go to bed.

Zach and Haley had shared a room up until three months ago when he said she talked too much as he tried to fall asleep. We needed another bedroom but this was all I could afford. I kissed Zach's forehead and pulled the blankets up to his neck. "What about stories, Mom?"

"Not tonight," I said.

"You didn't read last night, either."

"The tree pushed everything later tonight. I'll read extra books tomorrow," I said. He didn't look like he believed me and I didn't blame him. In his eyes I could see what I was becoming or failing to become. I kissed his head and crossed the hall to my bedroom to tuck Haley in bed.

She grabbed my hand before I could leave. "Go to bed now, Mom."

"I can't. I need to wash the dishes."

"Stay in here while I fall asleep. See," she said, closing her eyes, "I'm almost asleep already." I tried to pull my hand away. "Please, please," she said, keeping her eyes closed.

I slid into the bed next to her and sat on top of the comforter, running my finger over her forehead. I had no idea who she looked like. It wasn't Brad and she only had my hair but the rest of her belonged to someone else in the family, maybe my father. Too many times I looked at myself in the mirror wondering what parts of him I had inherited. I crept my fingers down Haley's arm and she smiled, pretending to sleep. I wondered how old she would be when the world would start working her over as it had done me and at what point her childlike innocence would end. Would it be during the next heated battle between Brad and me or later when some kid makes fun of her crooked teeth and lack of physical ability? When would she go through the door that lets in her future and would she be prepared? I watched her breathe and the crescent smile fell into a loose O. A collection of children's books and some of my favorite novels were stacked on my nightstand. I picked up *Pride and Prejudice* and looked at the bookmark. It was my third time reading the book but I had started this read three months ago. My heart raced at the thought of Ed and Brad and Christmas and I slid my legs off the bed. I kissed Haley's forehead and wished to be more like her: able to trust despite the news, able to laugh in spite of the failures, able to cheer despite the darkness, and able to believe in goodness in spite of the hazards in the road.

I walked to the kitchen and stood in the middle of it, staring at the mess on the countertops, the bills in the basket, the letter from Ed, and the off-white walls and white appliances. I was so tired of off-white walls and white appliances. My marriage had been off-white walls and white appliances — blah and nothing remarkable. I wanted color and radiance and a window to let in the light. I opened the drawer under the phone and pulled out a notepad and pen and wrote the Christmas letter I had long ago abandoned. *Dear God,* I wrote. *Please help me.*

I slid it into an envelope, placed it beneath the tree, and went to bed.

FIVE

Marshall listened as the phone rang in his ear. "Dwight, I'm three weeks from my anniversary. Can you order those flowers your gal showed me a few days ago?"

"Which ones did you want, Marshall?"

"The ones I couldn't pronounce along with all those others. And send a bouquet of mixed flowers to Judy. She'd rather have chocolate but flowers are healthier."

Dwight laughed. "What do you want on Judy's card?"

"Just write, *Hurry back before I shoot him.* She'll know what it means."

Marshall heard Dwight scribbling on the other end of the phone. "I'll have them ready on the twenty-third."

Marshall hung up the phone and pulled out the diamond necklace, letting it dangle off his fingers. Some people said he spoiled Linda but he always thought it was the other way around. He missed her voice and picked up the phone.

Gloria sorted through a stack of mail. "Christmas card from the Fuentes," she said. "Look, a cute picture of Luis." She held the picture in front of Miriam.

"I hope that child grows into his ears someday."

Gloria shoved the photo back inside the envelope. "Unfathomable. You're even rude at Christmas." She opened another envelope and gasped as she read the letter inside. "Oh, my," she said, looking around. "Oh, goodness." She put the card down on the table and leaned on her elbows, whispering, "What does this mean?"

Miriam snatched the card off the table, reading it. "Well, I'm not a rocket scientist but let me see if I can figure this out. 'Dear Gloria.' That's you. 'I have no idea how to tell you how fond I am of you. I think you are a perfectly lovely woman and if you are willing I would love the opportunity get to know you better.' There is no signature so I can only assume this is someone at the correctional institute who is trying to conceal his identity or a secret admirer." Gloria straightened her sweatshirt and pinned the unruly curls around her face to the side of her head. "Oh, stop trying to fix yourself up now. Whoever this is, he is painfully aware of what you look like." Miriam continued to read. " 'If you are willing, I was wondering if we could meet somewhere to talk? Please think about it. I will send another letter in a few days.' "

Gloria put her hands on top of her head and slunk down in her seat. "Whatever are you doing?" Miriam asked.

"I haven't been on a date in forty years! No wait!" Her fingers flew in front of her. "Forty-four years!"

Miriam hissed across the table. "Sit up right now. This is deplorable behavior for a grown woman."

"Good morning, ladies," I said, approaching their table. "Is something wrong?"

"Well," Miriam said, waving a letter in the air. "Gloria here has a secret admirer."

A twinge of sadness swept over me. I wanted that — that feeling of being pursued and needed in a way I wanted my children whenever I was away from them. I smiled and sounded excited. "That's awesome," I said, setting their coffee and tea on the table. "Do you have any idea who it could be?"

Gloria shook her head. "No. Never. Who would ever do such a . . . I've only dated one man my entire life. I need lipstick."

She dug through her purse and Miriam looked at me, shaking her head. "And what about your young buck?" she asked.

I began writing on the ordering pad. "There is no young buck," I said, cutting them off before they could ask about TS. I checked over what I had written. "Bacon, egg, and cheese on an onion bagel, and boiled egg, medium yolk, with dry wheat toast."

"Perfect," Gloria said. "You already know us so well. Scary, isn't it?"

I smiled and went to input their order. I felt badly for being so short with them. Four insurance agents at table six nodded for more coffee and I walked to their table faking a laugh at one's lame attempt to be charming. Sometimes I got so tired of this job.

Miriam hissed at me through her teeth and I turned to look at her. "TS is back," she said, keeping her voice low. A wave of heat spread across my face and my hands shook as I topped off Gloria's coffee.

Voices swarmed in my head. They were of Brad laughing and my mother telling me not to marry him and the voices of my own cynicism and failure. Then there was the voice that whispered, "Not yet. The dream isn't dead. I'm still here." But my own voice was too loud and drowned it out. I saw TS out of the corner of my eye but didn't dare acknowledge him. I set down the pitcher of cream and walked to the kitchen. "He's back," I said, whispering loudly to Karen. Aprons hung on the wall and I ran my hands through them.

"Who's back?" she asked, picking up an order.

I found an apron with a name tag and pulled it down, taking off the tag. "The guy from yesterday." I looked at her as I pinned the name to my uniform. "Do you think you could —"

"I can't right now," she said, cutting me off. "I'm slammed."

My throat was dry. Why was he back? What was he doing? I should have just taken the phone call from Brad last night instead of dealing with this today. I rushed around the corner to pick up three waters for my new tables. I greeted my customers then walked to table three, setting the water down in front of TS.

"So you have a name today?" he said.

I froze. "What?"

He pointed to the tag. "You didn't have your name tag yesterday." He leaned over to see it. "Rosemary." He paused. "You don't look like a Rosemary."

"My mother thought I did."

He threw his hands in the air. "I didn't mean anything by that. It's a beautiful name. I'm just glad to know your name today. I should have asked yesterday. My grandfather would be very disappointed." He smiled, wanting me to be charmed.

"What would you like?"

"Do you have any other recommendations for me?" He slid his arm up on the bench and I tapped my pen onto the ordering pad.

"I hear a boiled egg with dry wheat toast is good."

"I'll take it," he said. "What else do you recommend?"

He was smug and reminded me of Brad. "What are you doing here?"

He took his arm off the top of the bench. "I came here to eat."

"No, you didn't," I said.

He looked around and cast his eyes up at me. "Well, I was hoping you'd be working."

He was making fun of me. "Why'd you come in here?"

His back straightened and any charm he had been feeling fell cold to the table. "I was told to come here."

I snatched up the menu and walked away. Karen and Tasha were both too busy to help with his table but even if they weren't I knew I couldn't ask them again without appearing like an emotionally unstable divorced woman dragging her baggage to work every day. I was humiliated and felt so silly. Gloria's and Miriam's orders were up and I snatched them off the grill line, positioning parsley and orange slices on each plate. They were still reading their mail when I set their food in front of them. Gloria noticed my tag. "I thought you said your name was Christine."

"It is," I said, pretending to be having a normal conversation.

"Then why have you assumed the identity of a fifty-five-year-old pastry maker with arthritic knees?"

I smiled and refilled her coffee. "Because of my ex-husband. He sent in TS to see if I worked here."

I realized Craig or any one of the cooks would be calling my name any second for my other orders and I rushed to the back before they did. Craig placed the boiled egg and toast on a plate and I reached for it before he could call me. I ignored the orange slices and parsley and walked the plate to table three, putting it in front of TS. "Next time, just tell him to come in himself." He stared at me but didn't say a word. I didn't think he would.

■ ■ ■ ■

As TS was leaving he stepped to the display case and leaned toward the cash register. "Excuse me," he said. Tasha turned to look at him. "Does Christy work here?" The name shot through my head at the waitress station and I pushed a tray of drinks to the floor. Karen jumped and threw her hand to her chest; Tasha stepped away from the counter to reach for the broom and dustpan. TS smiled apologetically and left.

"What happened?" Betty said, stepping out of the kitchen.

"I'm sorry, Betty," I said. "I'll pay for these."

She watched me sweep up the glass and guide it into the dustpan. "Why are you wearing Rosemary's name tag?"

I dumped the shards of glass into the garbage and used the mop to soak up the water. Two days on the job and I was performing under par and looked like an idiot. "My ex-husband knew I lost my job at Patterson's and sent social services after me so he could threaten to take my kids again."

"Ah," Betty said, taking the mop from me. "I broke more than just a few glasses over my ex-husband," she said. "Just go to anger management before setting his motorcycle on fire."

"Did *you* do that?" I asked.

"I don't want to point fingers," she said. She reached for a cloth under the waitress station and wiped crumbs off the countertop. "Listen, I learned more than I wanted through my divorce." She used her thumbnail to pick at a crumb lodged in the seam of the counter. "And I realized that all the sniping, whining, and guerilla tactics took a lot of nine-to-five energy." She stopped and looked at me. "All of my defensive maneuvers didn't change the fact that I had two children to take care of and the more I fought and argued the more I hurt them because they weren't getting me; they were getting this pumped up, caustic, aggressive version of me. Does that make sense?"

I wanted to say, "Yes! Yes! That's me," but settled for nodding my head.

She crouched down and cleaned the baseboards under the display case. "Of course by the time I figured that out I had an angry teenager on my hands. He didn't like me or his father and I couldn't blame him. He took a detour that lasted many years but that's a whole other story." She stood up and smiled at me. "I don't know your ex,

Christine. I have no idea what he's like but . . . all I'm saying is don't let it consume you."

"I don't think it is," I said.

She smiled. "It is, doll. You think some kid has been sent in here to spy on you."

I realized how ludicrous it sounded. "I know it sounds far-fetched but Brad would do that."

She crossed her arms and her eyes scrunched up when she smiled. "Why? To prove that you're here working during the middle of the day while your kids are at school? How could he use that against you?" I didn't have an answer. She put her hands on my shoulders and patted them hard. "You remind me so much of my grand-daughter so I'm going to say this. Take it from an old gal who traveled this same road a long time ago. If you don't stop looking over your shoulder and really notice what's happening to you and around you and inside of you then you're going to run the risk of losing what's most important to you."

Jason finished the disappointing call with his headhunter. "Keep your head up," Louis said. "Christmas is never a good time to be looking for work. But there are plenty of firms out there that will be hiring in the

New Year."

"Give me a call if something turns up," Jason said before hanging up the phone.

Marshall waited until Jason was off the phone before handing him another quiz.

Jason sighed, looking at him. "You know I always get the first nine questions right, so to save both of us time why don't you just ask me number ten?"

"Fair enough," Marshall said. "What's the lady's name who's in charge of the janitorial staff?"

Jason laughed. "How about, who are the ladies in cosmetics and jewelry or the guy in shoes who walks with a limp?" Marshall shook his head. "You know I have rent to pay, right?"

"I do. And if —" Jason got up in a huff and walked to the office door. "Where are you going?"

"Looking for the cleaning lady," Jason said.

"Hey, wait!" Marshall said. "Where're my cookies?"

"I didn't get any."

Marshall hung his jacket on the coatrack. "Why not?"

"Because Rosemary said to come in yourself."

Marshall folded his arms and stared at

him. "What?"

"Yeah. I don't know what you did but you really ticked her off," Jason said.

"And she said I couldn't have my white chocolate chip macadamias?"

"She said next time you need to go in yourself. And I have a feeling when you do she's going to rip into you like a monkey on a cookie."

Marshall stepped toward his office. "Of all the crazy things."

"Is she single?" Jason said, holding the office door open.

"She's a widow, actually."

"A widow?" He let the door rest on his backside. "When did her husband die?"

"Long before I knew her," Marshall said.

"How long have you known her?"

Marshall thought for a moment. "At least five years." Jason nodded and Marshall watched him. "Why are you asking so many questions about Rosemary?"

Jason shrugged. "I don't know. There's something about her."

"About *Rosemary?*"

"Karen, are you interested in working a double?" Betty asked. "Maddie is sick and can't work today."

"I'll do it," I said, realizing I was stepping

out of bounds. I looked at Karen. "I'm sorry. I meant if you don't want to work it that I could."

Karen filled her tray with glasses of ice water and looked at Betty. "If Christine wants it she can have it."

"The shift starts at four thirty," Betty said.

My mind kicked into gear. I needed to find a sitter. I left messages for both Allie and Mira and racked my brain for the name of the place the social worker had mentioned when she came to the house. It finally came to me and I dialed information for the number to Glory's Place. "Please be open," I said, dialing the number.

"Glory's Place. This is Heddy," a woman said.

"Hi. My name's Christine and I got your name from" — I didn't want to tell her a social worker who had made a visit — "a friend. I have a seven-year-old and a five-year-old who need supervision after school. Is there any way I could drop them off today?"

"I'm sorry. We are maxed out right now after school. I can take down your name and number and let you know when we have some openings."

I gave her my information but hung up with little hope that they'd ever be able to

144

help. I opened the directory in my cell phone and scrolled down it. A name popped out at me and I dialed the number, listening as it rang in my ear.

"Hello." I was so relieved to hear that voice.

"Renee!"

"Christine! How are you, kid? How's the new job?"

"It's great but I'm in a jam," I said. I hated that I didn't have time to catch up with her and realized I was sounding short and uninterested in her life. "I have the chance to work a double tonight and I need to work it to buy the kids' presents and pay rent and —"

She cut me off. "I'll watch your kids. What time?"

"Are you sure, Renee? What about Sherman?"

"A night away will make that man appreciate me for all the ways I keep him fed and organized and walking straight."

What a relief. I watched a table of four sit down in my section. "I miss working with you, Renee."

"I'll let you know how I feel about you after I take care of your kids." I laughed and dropped the phone into my apron pocket.

■ ■ ■ ■

The lunch crowd fell off by two o'clock. I cashed in my tips and Betty handed me sixty-two dollars and seventy cents. Hopefully, I could make more than that at dinner. The strange "day-old pastry lady" slid into a booth by the window and I put a cup of black coffee on my tray. "Hi," I said, setting it in front of her.

"Hi." Her eyes were sunken and black with lack of rest. She had a red nose and blue fingers from walking here and held the cup between her hands to get warm.

"Have you found a job?" She shook her head. "Can I get you anything to eat?"

"No. Just the coffee and a day-old pastry."

I wondered if she didn't eat because she wasn't hungry or if she felt that she shouldn't eat. She not only didn't look well but seemed to have long lost touch with what being well meant. "All the day-olds are gone," I said. "There weren't many today." She nodded and looked out the window. She always seemed somewhere that was unreachable and distant, someplace far beyond the restaurant window. "Do you live around here?" I asked, resting the tray on my hip. She nodded. "Where?"

She set her cup down and looked out the window. "I'm not looking for friends, okay? Just coffee and pastry."

Renee and I spent too little time catching up when I got home but I was zapped. After she left I crept into Zach's room and sat on the edge of his bed, touching his leg. What would I do without him and Haley? What would I be without them? I watched him breathe and knew in that half-lit bedroom what I lacked and what I failed to give my children. I sensed it was what the coffee-and-pastry-lady desired more than anything else and what she would give to taste it. It was a whisper in the soul, a lump in the throat, and an echo in the deep and hidden places of the heart. It was the hope that we are loved, truly loved, and that we are known. It was what I wanted more than anything.

Six

Marshall swung open the door to Betty's and shivered as the heat touched his skin. He pulled off his gloves and walked to the display case. "Is Rosemary working today?" he asked, peering into the case of baked goods.

"Yep," Tasha said. "Rosemary!" Rosemary glanced up from her work in the kitchen and saw Marshall through the window that divided the kitchen and dining hall. She set aside a lump of dough and stepped around the corner to the counter.

"Hi, Marshall," she said, smiling. "How are you today?"

"Well, I'm great. I was wondering how you were."

She brushed the flour from her hands onto the apron. "I'm doing fine," she said, looking at him.

He fumbled for words. "You're sure you're okay?"

"Yes. Did you hear otherwise? Have you been talking to my doctor?" she said, laughing.

"No, no. I just thought . . . you know . . . that maybe you needed to see me."

She leaned onto the counter. "About what?" she said, whispering.

"About the cookies," he said.

Her face bordered on confusion and laughter. "Did you get a bad batch?" she said, leaning closer. "Too much salt? Too hard?"

He shook his head. "No, every cookie I've ever eaten here has been great. I'd actually love a sack if that's okay."

"Sure," she said. "I don't normally work the cash register but Tasha could help you. Do you need anything else, Marshall?"

"No, do you?"

Rosemary looked at him, puzzled. "No. I'm fine."

"Well, great! Good to see you." He waved as she walked back to the kitchen. Tasha handed him a sack of white chocolate chip macadamia cookies and Marshall stuck his nose inside the bag and picked out a cookie, sighing as he smelled it.

Patricia Addison moved a half-empty cup of cold coffee to Roy Braedon's desk and smiled. She'd been putting partially eaten donuts, cups with coffee dregs on the bottom, and candy wrappers on his desk for years and it drove him crazy. Her phone rang and she reached for it. "This is Patricia."

"This is Brad Eisley." Patricia couldn't place the name right away. "You went to my ex-wife's house but you never called me back."

Patricia picked up a pen and her notepad, remembering. "I filed my report, Mr. Eisley."

"But I didn't see it."

"Your attorney has access to those files."

"But they're my kids. They come home from school and aren't supervised. They're being neglected. Your report shows that, right?"

Patricia cringed. "My report is an accurate documentation of what I witnessed in the home and after spending time with the children."

He paused. "So what does that mean?"

"Your attorney can share the information with you, Mr. Eisley. Thank you for calling." She hung up and turned to see Roy, standing at his desk. "Do you ever get the feeling that some people have a need to be a jerk? They just can't get through the day without being a jerk to someone. It doesn't matter who: the bus driver maybe, or the cashier at the grocery store, the guy they work with, or the ex-wife, for whatever reason. He just wakes up and says, 'It's a new day. I must be a jerk.' "

Roy took a bite of a bagel and wiped cream cheese from his chin. "What'd I do now?" Patricia laughed and leaned forward, picking up the phone. "Who are you calling?" he asked. "Are you getting ready to stir the pot?"

"No," she said, listening as the phone rang in her ear. "I'm taking the pot off the stove. Gloria! It's Patricia." Gloria had been a foster mother for many of Patricia's cases and the women had developed a close relationship over the years.

"Give me the mother's information," Gloria said. "Someone will get in touch with her in the next couple of days."

Clayton came in but without Julie or the kids. He sat at a booth with another man and I approached them with coffee. "No Ava and Adam today?" I asked.

"No," he said, putting the cup to his lips. I took their orders and walked to the computer.

"How's Clayton's wife?" Karen asked.

"I didn't know anything was wrong with her," I said.

"She has cancer."

Julie was young. Her children were young. Her husband had just ordered an omelet with bacon, onion, and cheese. How could she have cancer? I made my way around my tables and refilled every one's coffee, stopping at Clayton's booth. "How's Julie?" I asked.

"She's doing better," he said. "Last week was hard. The chemo made her so sick and now her hair's falling out but this week she feels stronger. Her sister came into town and took her for her treatment today." His voice was full and warm and in love with her. Craig called my name and I ran to get their orders hoping I'd never see Clayton without Julie again.

Jason piled armloads of shirts and dress slacks onto rolling carts and wheeled them into the men's department. He noticed a small boy hiding in the middle of one of the circular racks and leaned over the top of it to peer down at him. "Hey, there," he said. "What are you doing?"

"This is my command post," the boy said.

"Like for a mission?" Jason asked, guessing the boy to be around five.

The boy nodded. "Space mission. I'm the commander. You be the bad guy."

"No can do," Jason said. "I'm working and the boss man gets real mad if I don't do my job."

"What's your name?" the boy asked.

"Jason. What's yours?"

"Marcus," the boy said, peering his face out between the slacks. "I'm four."

"What the hell are you doing?" a young black man asked, yanking the boy from out of the middle of the rack.

"Playing space mission," Marcus said.

"Damn it, Marcus. I told you to stay by me," the man said. He looked no older than Jason.

"He was okay," Jason said. "He wasn't bothering anything."

"He's always bothering things," the man said, jerking the boy's arm. "Get out of there." He turned to look at Jason. "I need khaki pants for a job. You got any?"

Jason pointed to a table. "They're all stacked right there. More sizes in the back."

"Don't go anywhere," the man said to Marcus.

Marcus looked up and Jason shrugged his shoulders. "Your dad's kind of mad," Jason said.

"He's not my dad," Marcus said. "He's

153

my mom's boyfriend. The other one left."

"Hey, come back sometime and we'll play space mission," Jason said, whispering. "Next time I'll be Dakmar the Dark from the planet Gondor and I'll threaten your planet with total ruin and devastation."

"What's ruin and debastation?" Marcus asked.

"It's bad," Jason said. "It's really, really bad!"

The man paid Matt for his pants and grabbed Marcus's hand. "Come on," he said.

"Bye," Marcus said, waving.

"Idiot," Jason said, watching the man walk ahead of Marcus through the store.

"Have you gone to Glory's Place yet?" Marshall asked.

Jason jumped at his voice and tugged on the rack, pulling it to the front of the department. "No."

Matt busied himself tearing apart the denim display and pretended not to listen. "But it'd be good for you," Marshall said, perturbed.

"I think I know what's good for me," Jason said, hanging several button-down shirts onto a rack.

Marshall lifted a handful of shirts and added them to the rack. "Is what you do for your own good or for someone else's good as well?"

Jason rolled his eyes. It sounded like a plaque on one of the office walls. "All I'm saying is I don't want to volunteer there. I'm not rejecting all of mankind here."

Marshall grabbed the sleeves of several shirts and shook out the wrinkles. "We help Glory's Place every year with donations but they need help from young people like you."

Jason's phone beeped and he pulled it out of his pocket, reading a text message from Ashley. Marshall held out his hand. "What?" Jason said.

"Absolutely no phones on the floor."

"I'm not talking to anyone. I'm reading a text."

"Not on store time you're not." He held his open palm in front of Jason. Jason smirked and put the phone in Marshall's hand. "Pick it up on your break."

Jason swore beneath his breath and Matt stepped from behind the denim wall he was building. "What's wrong?" he asked.

"He took my phone. Good news is I read the text and my girlfriend's coming here for a visit."

"I didn't know you had a girlfriend," Matt said.

"If she's coming for a visit she'll be my

girlfriend," Jason said.

"So it's all about convenience and timing?" Matt asked.

"That's the way it usually plays out," Jason said.

On Friday Maddie was diagnosed with pneumonia and I asked Betty if I could work her shift until she came back. She agreed and I scrambled again to find a sitter. By two thirty I still hadn't found one and the kids would be home in an hour and a half. I would have an hour off between my first and second shift. I reasoned that if I hadn't found someone by then that I would race home and make something for Zach and Haley's dinner. I didn't tell anyone what I was thinking, that for the first time in their lives my children would stay home alone. *If I make dinner, cover the window on the front door so no one can see inside, and they lock the door then they'll be safe,* I said to myself. *They can eat, do their homework, watch a movie, and then it'll be time for bed. No, they can't do that. They're too little.* I battled with myself until three thirty and then bolted out the door for home.

Leftover tuna casserole was in the fridge and I poured some peas into a bowl with a little water and popped it in the microwave. I reached for a plate and scooped three big spoonfuls of casserole onto it. While the peas cooked I went to the bathroom and pulled out a bath towel. I tried to secure it over the front door window but it was too heavy and I had no way to hold it there. I ran for the kitchen and brought out the roll of paper towels and the masking tape. I hung three sheets of towel over the first window and three over the second, securing each "curtain" with the tape. I hung a second and third layer on each window and taped the bottom of the towels as well, holding them in place. I opened the door and stepped outside, trying to peer through the windows. "There," I said. I shut the blinds on the living-room windows and pulled the curtain to cover the deck sliding door. I checked the blinds in each of the bedrooms and ran back to the living room to make sure the TV and DVD player were all set for a movie. *They'll be okay,* I thought, warming the tuna casserole. *They'll be okay, they'll be okay, they'll be okay.*

The phone rang and I jumped. I popped the second plate in the microwave and pushed start. "Hello," I said.

"Uh, hi. Is this Angela Eisley?" a man asked.

I always knew when it was a telemarketer because they always called me by my first name. I reached for the aluminum foil. I had no time for salespeople right now. "It is but —"

"My name's Jason and I'm calling with Glory's Place."

I ripped off a sheet of aluminum foil and wrapped it around the warm plate. "Right! Yes," I said.

"Um, I was told to call you and let you know that Glory's Place has room for your children if you need to bring them in sometime after school."

I let out a sigh of relief. "You are a lifesaver," I said. "I really didn't think I'd ever hear from you again. When can I bring them?"

I heard him talking with someone in the background. "The center is closed on Tuesdays and Thursdays but you can bring them the other days."

"Do I need to tell you when I'm bringing Zach and Haley or can I just drop them off?"

I heard more muffled mumbling in the background. "You can just drop them off. Come in and fill out paperwork with whoever's here. Usually Dalton and Heddy are here in the afternoon."

My mind kicked into gear to find a sitter for Tuesday. The microwave beeped and I ripped off another sheet of aluminum foil. "You have no idea how you've made my day," I said.

"Well, that's what I try to do," he said. "It's my gift."

I heard screaming at the door and thanked the man for calling again. Zach and Haley fell into the doorway, breathing hard. "She's standing there again, Mom!" Zach said, handing me his coat.

"Who? Mrs. Meredith?"

"You mean the Bat Lady," Haley said, kicking off her boots.

"Please don't let her hear you call her that," I said. "It's not nice."

"Bats aren't nice, either," Zach said.

I squatted down and pulled each of them in front of me. "Listen, we need to talk," I said.

Jason input Angela's information into the computer and stepped out of the office at Glory's Place. He saw a little boy trying to shoot a basket and walked to the court. "Hey! Space commander!"

Marcus turned and smiled. "Hey, I know you. You're Dakmar the Great."

"Dakmar the *Dark*. And don't you forget

it," Jason said. "What are you doing here?"

"His mother dropped him off at our house this morning," Dalton said. Dalton Gregory and his wife Heddy had been instrumental in finding this building for Glory's Place. Gloria kept them busy but they never complained. "It beats the alternative," Dalton always said.

"Hey, Jason! Watch this." Jason turned as Marcus popped a basketball high above his head.

"Nothing but air," Jason said. "What was that? Here, try it like this." He helped Marcus hold the ball and send it flying.

"It's hard," Marcus said.

"But it gets easier. You just need to practice." He laughed, watching Marcus heave the ball. "It's not a shot put. It's a ball!" Marcus laughed and tried again. "Why's he here?" Jason asked.

Dalton removed some boxes from the top of a cafeteria table and set them on the floor. He kept his voice low. "His mother's live-in slaps her around. She's been to the women's rescue mission several times but she always goes back to him."

"Why?" Jason asked, helping Dalton move the boxes to the floor.

Dalton shrugged. "Why do they ever go back? I don't know. She started a new job today and didn't want to leave Marcus home with him."

"I saw him with Marcus in the store. I wouldn't leave him alone with him, either. Has he ever hit Marcus?"

"Not that we know of but after a night of drinking or drugs that could change."

Jason watched Marcus pop the ball into the air again and cheered when it swished the bottom of the net. "Now you're talking," he said. "Another six inches and it's going in." Marcus smiled and ran for the ball. "Would you need me tomorrow?" he asked.

"Absolutely," Dalton said. He pointed to two tables covered with boxes. "All these boxes need to be filled along with those against the wall. We're waiting for the box of donations from Wilson's along with a box of shampoo, toothpaste, and toothbrushes from the grocery store." Dalton walked to the next table and began stacking the boxes onto the floor. "We're going to need this space when the donations come in."

Jason picked up a stack of four boxes and set them on the floor. "Who are the boxes for?"

"The homeless and all the families we help here."

Jason pulled his cap over his head. "Did

Gloria start this place?"

"Out of the back of her car," Dalton said. "Her son was missing for seven years and she couldn't stand the thought of him wandering the street, wondering if anyone was helping him. She opened her trunk and started passing out socks. It grew from there."

Jason looked around the space with the bright-colored walls, classroom area with a few tables and folding chairs, small kitchen space with a few cabinets, refrigerator, and countertop, and the play area complete with indoor basketball hoop, jump ropes, balls, and Marcus, and something moved him. It wasn't a voice. It wasn't loud; it fell more like mist but Jason ignored it. "It doesn't look like much but a lot happens here," Dalton said.

"How long have you been here?" Jason asked, walking toward the front door.

"We've been in this space for two years and before that we operated out of Gloria's home for several years."

"And the kids who come here?"

"Most are being raised by a single mother or their grandparents. Most of them don't have an active father. A lot of them like Marcus don't even know their father." He called to Marcus and held his coat out for

162

him. "Let's go home and see what Heddy is making for dinner."

"I hope it's mac and cheese!" Marcus said.

"I hope it's not," Dalton said, zipping the boy's coat.

"You coming tomorrow?" Marcus asked, looking at Jason.

"I'll be here," Jason said, holding out his fist for Marcus to bump it.

"I'm gonna take you down, Dakmar," Marcus said.

"That's big talk from a kid who can't even get the ball to the rim!"

Jason wrapped his scarf around his neck and stuck his hands in his pocket for the walk back to Wilson's. His steps were quick over the sidewalks that were whitening with snow but he heard that voice inside him again or was it an echo or something else? It was falling without a sound like light or flakes of snow. He pushed it away. He loved accounting; he was convinced he did it with heart and not just for the paycheck. High-rise living in the city is what he was made for, not some garage apartment in this place. He had *no* desire to live here or shoot hoops with Marcus after school. The kid couldn't offer him anything anyway. He reasoned that the sky was too bright, the air too cold, and his belly too hungry to think clearly. There wasn't a voice among the barren crab apple trees or whispers among the dormant daylilies. He saw the sign for Betty's up ahead and bent his head down to avoid the snow. He'd get something to eat and forget about Glory's Place.

Betty hugged a young woman and waved at someone waiting in a car in front of the restaurant. She closed the door and smiled when she saw me. "Oh, I wish you'd been here thirty seconds earlier to meet my granddaughter! She and her mother come into town and stay with me this time every year and we eat too much food and stay up too late talking."

I followed her to the counter and leaned onto it. "So, was that your daughter in the car?"

Betty slipped on a plastic glove and arranged the pastries in the display case and put any broken cookies into a plastic bag. "Daughter-in-law. She married my son."

I grabbed the bottle of window cleaner and sprayed the top of the display case, shining it. "Did he ever work here with you?"

She laughed. "When he was a teenager he absolutely refused to work in the restaurant with me. His girlfriend did but not Dennis.

He thought he was too good. He wasted a lot of years around that time. Did too many drugs. Lost too many jobs. Used too many people. But he finally came to his senses as they say." She was quiet and closed the display case. "He met Maureen and one day he said he'd like to work in the bakery. He was the best baker in the city." She looked down into the case and smiled. "He came up with most of these pastry recipes. Nobody makes a cream cheese bear claw as good as Betty's Bakery and that's because of Dennis."

"So why'd he stop working here?" I asked, setting out two new stacks of napkins in the basket on top of the counter.

"Heart attack eight years ago. Took him like that," she said, snapping her fingers. "They said he didn't feel any pain. It's always easier on the one leaving." She held the bag of cookie pieces out to me. "For your babies." She saw a longtime customer enter with her grandson and walked around the corner to greet her. Since I had started at Betty's I wondered what it was about this short, stout woman that made her so endearing. I thought it was because she had caught something from her son's passing. It flickered out through her in the way she talked with customers or dealt with employees. She wasn't given over to sentimental hogwash, she was too realistic for that, nor did she romanticize anyone's problems. They were what they were and Betty understood. That kind of compassion comes with living and losing what you love. I had the sense that Betty had lost a lot.

Zach and Haley crouched against the wall in his bedroom and listened as the knock grew louder and louder. "It must be the Bat Lady," Haley said, whispering. "I can hear her flapping her wings."

"Shh," Zach said, scolding her. "We don't want her to know we're in here."

"I don't like being here without Mom," Haley said, clutching Brown Dog tighter to her chest.

The phone began to ring and Haley jumped up. "Sit down," Zach said, whispering. "We can't answer that. We'd have to run out to the kitchen and the Bat Lady would hear us and know we're in here." The knocking and ringing bounced off the walls and Haley covered her ears.

I opened my cell phone and tried calling the kids again. *They're all right,* I thought. *They're just busy playing and didn't hear the phone.* It rang several times and my heart beat faster. "Oh, God," I whispered. "Please." It clicked to voice mail and I snapped the phone shut.

"You have a table," Betty said, leaning around the corner.

"I'm coming," I said, dialing the phone again. *Come on, baby. Come on.*

"Hello." Zach's voice was quiet and I wanted to cry.

"Zach, I've been calling. Where are you?"

"We were in my bedroom because someone was knocking on the door. It was probably the Bat Lady trying to scare us."

I didn't know if I should laugh or cry. "Mrs. Meredith wouldn't bother you," I said. "Take the phone to your bedroom while you play and remember to see if it's me before you answer it."

"Okay, Mom. Are you coming home now?"

"No, honey. I have a few more hours to go." He was quiet on the other end. "Great job not answering the door. What was your sister doing?"

"Freaking out."

I laughed. "Good job keeping her calm. Why don't you take three cookies each back to your room?"

"How about four each?"

At that point I would have let them eat

the whole package. "You bet. I love you, big man." He was quiet. "Zach?"

"I've got the hand signal up for I love you."

I laughed and hung up. I didn't know how I would keep my mind on work for the next five hours. How could I have left them home alone? My phone vibrated and I glanced down to see if it was Zach. It was Brad. I ignored it. I glanced at my section and noticed TS sitting at table one. I could hear Gloria in my head: "He's TO today. Like Toto."

I didn't have the mental energy to give him much thought; my mind was at home with Zach and Haley. "Hi," I said, setting a glass of water in front of him.

"I thought you worked mornings," he said, taking off his coat.

"I'm working a double today."

He seemed awkward and tongue-tied. "I told my grandfather to come in." I looked at him, confused. "Did he? He said he talked to you." I had no idea what he meant. "He had a sack of cookies so I know he came in."

"Sure," I said, just following along. "He bought cookies."

"So everything's good again?" His hair stuck out from beneath his cap and he looked like an ad in one of the outdoor magazines my grandfather would read.

"Yes," I said. I was puzzled but he was so sincere about it that I found him charming. Betty busied herself sweeping beneath nearby tables and I wondered if she was spying on me. I looked over at her and she nodded her head toward TS, winking. I rolled my eyes and looked back at him. "What would you like?"

He glanced over the menu. "Well, I'd ask you but I'm afraid you'd recommend a boiled egg with dry toast again." I smiled. "Could I just have a burger?"

"Fries or onion rings?"

"Surprise me," he said. I was smiling over *that. Come on,* I said to myself. "Hey," he said as I turned to walk away. "How long have you lived here?"

"Seven years."

"Is this what you wanted? You know, when you were a kid?"

I thought a moment and wondered what he was getting at. "No," I said. "It's different."

"In a good way or in a bad way?"

"In a different way," I said, thinking out loud. I walked to the waitress station and was aware of my jeans and the apron around my waist and hoped he wasn't looking at me again. Betty winked and put her thumb in the air. He was.

"So the spy is back," she said, whispering as I input his order. "Do you think he's FBI or CIA?" I smiled and pretended to ignore her. "Or do you think he has his own private investigation firm? Somebody batten down those glasses," she said over her shoulder. "Things could start flying here any minute."

I laughed and reached for a glass. "Okay, he's not a spy."

"Of course he's not," she said. "But he is awfully cute, isn't he?"

"I haven't noticed," I said. I stepped around the corner to call home and noticed Brad had tried calling again. "What do you want now?" I said, looking at the phone. He didn't leave a message. I dialed the house and waited. Haley answered. "Are you okay?" I asked.

"Can I have chips?"

They were fine. "Did you eat all your casserole and peas?"

"There's one noodle and one pea left on my plate."

"Fill one of the bright blue cups up but no more than that, okay?" She hung up and I imagined they'd eat from every bag and package before I got home.

I filled a glass with tea and took it to TS.

"So," he said. "What do you do for fun around here?"

Besides work, I hadn't been out of the house in ages. "I stay in mostly."

"So you like to what? Watch movies? Read?"

"Both," I said.

He put his arm over the chair and looked up at me. "What's your favorite book?"

"Too many to mention."

"Favorite movie?"

"Again, too many to mention but no horror or teen flicks."

"Aren't they one and the same?" he said. "What's your favorite color?"

"Purple."

"Favorite bug?"

"Favorite bug?" I asked, laughing.

"Yeah, which bug do you find most interesting?"

"The butterfly."

"Purple butterfly?"

"Of course." I touched my hair and pushed it behind my ear. What did it look like this afternoon? Did I have any lipstick left?

"What's your favorite flower?"

"Hydrangea."

"No kidding? My grandfather buys those all the time. What's your favorite site?"

"Kites in the sky," I said.

His mouth dropped open. "I figured you'd say the gondolas in Venice or Niagara Falls or the Eiffel Tower."

"I've never been to those places," I said, laughing. "Why so many questions?"

He took a drink of tea. "It's my grandfather's fault."

"I have no idea what that means."

"It's a good thing," he said, waving his hands in the air. "It's not creepy and weird."

I waited on my other tables and took their orders but was ever aware that TS was watching me as I moved around the dining room but I was okay with it. He was young and I was a mother. We could be friends. That would be fine. He finished his burger and ordered a piece of peanut butter pie. When that was finished he ordered a piece of hummingbird cake. "Someone doesn't want to leave," Betty said, wiping crumbs from the front counter. I knew he didn't want to leave and that pleased me to no end. I loved looking at and talking with him.

"Do you want any other desserts?" I asked, holding his bill in front of me.

"I didn't want the cake," he said. He smiled at me and I laughed. "Hey." He stopped and moved the last bite of cake around on his plate. "Is there any chance you'd like to go out with me sometime? To watch a non-horror, non-teen movie? Or maybe go to a bookstore and pick up one of the titles that are too many to mention?"

My heart sank. For all he knew I was single. No kids. No obligations. He was probably looking for fun and I wasn't much of that anymore. "Um."

"I know I came across as a jerk the day we met. I never even asked you your name until the second day. That says a lot. I know."

"No," I said. "It's not that at all. It's just that I work quite a bit now because . . ."

"If you're tired we can just sit and have coffee and pie one night," he said. "I guess that's not really all that appealing when you work in a restaurant that's known for coffee and pie."

I laughed and he smiled. I really loved that smile. "Coffee would be nice."

"How about the bookstore?"

"The bookstore would be nice, too," I said, tucking my hair behind my ear again.

He stood and put on his coat. "When?"

"I'll need to check my schedule. I'm try-ing to work a double shift as much as I can right now."

He handed me a twenty dollar bill. "I'll be back tomorrow. Does that give you time to check your schedule?"

I nodded and he walked toward the entrance. "You need change," I said.

"No, I don't," he said, pulling the hat over his ears. He left and I realized I didn't tell him about Zach and Haley. *Idiot,* I said to myself.

"So?" Betty asked, stepping next to me as I cashed out his bill.

"So he wants to do coffee," I said.

"And all the cards are out on the table? You told him you have children?" I shook my head. "But he does know your name is Christine, right?" I slammed the cash register drawer closed and snapped my head to look at her. Betty laughed and grabbed her coat off the rack to go home. "You are a piece of work," she said, reminding me of my grandmother.

"I was going to tell him about my kids. I forgot all about my name!"

"Now it's just going to be weird and awkward." She wrapped a neon pink scarf around her neck. "The truth shall set you free, you know."

I got home at nine thirty and found the house was a mess. Every couch cushion and throw pillow was on the floor in a circle with two or three books on top of each one. I had no idea what the kids had been playing. I found Zach and Haley together in his bed. I sat on the edge of the bed and Zach smiled with his eyes closed. "Faker," I said, whispering.

"She was afraid to sleep by herself," he said, pushing Haley's leg off of him.

"I sure am glad to see you," I said. "Were you okay?"

"You called a million times," he said, rubbing an eye with his index finger. "I could never play computer games because I'd be in the middle of a game when the phone would ring."

I laughed out loud. "Sorry! You did a great job keeping your sister safe." He nodded. "Was it scary?"

"Kind of," he said. "Especially when somebody kept knocking."

I played with his hair and he closed his eyes. "On Monday you're going to go to Glory's Place."

"What's that?"

"A really cool place where you can play basketball and lots of games and be with other kids. Sound good?"

He closed his eyes. "Sure." I kissed his forehead and his mouth fell open. He was asleep. I kissed Haley hard on her cheek and she never moved. "Thank you," I said, whispering.

SEVEN

Clayton and Julie sat at their favorite table. Julie's head was covered with a purple and teal wrap. Her blue eyes sparkled as I delivered coffee to them. Clayton led Ava and Adam to the counter and they pointed at the fresh cakes and cookies on display. "Glad to see you back this week," I said to Julie. "You look great."

"I feel great," she said. "I just have one more chemo treatment and then I start radiation."

"How are the kids?" I asked.

"Well, we kept it from them as long as we could. I didn't look sick so we didn't want to scare them. But now that my hair is nearly gone it's kind of hard to cover that up anymore. We just tell them that doctors are helping to take away a lump in my chest, and I ask them to help me pick a scarf out of the drawer every day."

"How are you getting through it?" I asked,

afraid after the fact that I was getting too personal.

"Hope," she said, watching her children. She wasn't wistful; her voice didn't break or fail her. It was simply all she had and she said it as if reading off her grocery list: eggs, bread, sugar, hope. It was just part of the deal. If she was afraid, Julie didn't show it and I didn't ask her. Clayton returned to the table and set a cupcake in front of Ava and a cookie in front of Adam. I glanced at Julie and she smiled. "I think I've gone soft," she said, watching Ava lick frosting off the cupcake. "But some things aren't a big deal, you know." She ran her finger through the frosting and licked it, smiling at Ava. Julie's hair was gone but her heart was full. A huge scar ran across her chest where her breast had been, but her love was complete. Poison was pushing through her body each week, but a hope beyond my own reason was pulling her through.

I input their orders and noticed Gloria and Miriam sitting down. I carried coffee and tea to their booth and watched as they pored over the morning's mail. "Anything in there from mystery man?" I asked.

"Nothing today," Miriam said, squeezing lemon into her tea. "But she did get a note a couple of days ago that said he'd like to

178

meet her Thursday in Ashton Gardens, but she won't even go and spy him out."

"He'd know either one of our cars and would see us making giant fools out of ourselves," Gloria said.

"I'll drive," I said.

The coffee-and-pastry lady sat in a booth by the window on Monday and her over-sized coat dwarfed her. She looked so sad and small. "Morning," I said, placing a cup of coffee in front of her.

She took the cup between her hands. "Hi."

"Any luck finding work?" I'm not sure why I kept trying to have a conversation with her. She shook her head. "Would you like a day-old today?"

She looked into her cup and nodded. "That'd be great. Maybe I'll buy two today. It's my birthday." Her eyes were full of mist and sorrow and regrets and she took a sip of coffee.

"Happy birthday!" I said. "So how young are you?"

She half-smiled but didn't answer me. I left her alone and walked to the baker's racks to find a day-old pastry but stopped, looking at the cakes. I picked up a chocolate one with butter cream frosting. "Hey, Karen," I said. "Can Stephanie or Rosemary write happy birthday on this cake?"

She stepped to my side and looked at it. "One of them probably could. Why?"

I nodded toward the pastry lady. "It's her birthday."

Karen reached in her apron and handed me a five dollar bill. "Here. To help pay for it." She glanced at Tasha. "If we all pitch in we can do something nice today."

"I don't even know that woman," Tasha said. I moved toward the kitchen and Tasha yelled after me, "Here!" She thrust two dollars toward me and sighed. "I have textbooks to buy you know!"

Rosemary wasn't in the kitchen but Stephanie was folding dough over tiny globs of jelly in the center of pastries. "Stephanie, can you write on a cake?"

She looked at it and frowned. "I can't even read my own writing," she said.

"What do you need?" Betty said, entering the kitchen from her office.

"Happy birthday," I said.

"Happy birthday who?" she asked, picking up a pastry bag.

I leaned my head toward the kitchen window that looked out over the dining room. "I don't know her name."

"That little gal who comes in here for coffee?" I nodded. She took the cake from me and grabbed a pastry bag filled with icing. Betty's hands were quick and graceful. I watched as she wrote the words and squeezed flowers out here and there on top of the cake. "Thanks!" I said, picking it up from the table.

"Hold on," she said. She walked to the grill and placed two slices of French toast onto a plate along with a side of fruit.

"That was Karen's order," Craig said.

"For Brewster," Betty said. "He can wait an extra two minutes. He should be ordering oatmeal anyway." She handed the plate to me and said, "Tell her it's on the house."

I turned the corner, holding the cake in one hand and the plate of French toast in the other. "Karen," I said, whispering. I kept my back to the counter so the woman wouldn't see what I had. "Can you help me sing?"

"Oh, please no," she said. "I hate those kind of restaurants. We're not one of those restaurants."

"Can we be for one minute?" I asked. "Tasha? Would you help, too? That lady's always alone. I have a feeling that if we don't do this then no one will."

Tasha closed the cash register and rolled her eyes. "Like I'm going to say no now. Just make it fast. Not one of those slow, drawn-out versions."

They walked in front of me to hide the cake. When we got to the table I stepped out front and we started to sing. The woman was surprised and embarrassed, partly by our singing I think. We sounded like sheep stuck between the rails of a fence. Gloria and Miriam and the customers around her sang along with us and we all stopped when we got to the name. We had no idea what to sing. "Tamara," she said, whispering. We finished the song and everyone clapped, because it was over, I'm sure!

"Happy birthday," Karen said before running to one of her tables.

Tasha set the French toast in front of her. "It's on the house," she said.

Tamara stared at the food. "Thank you," she said.

I picked up the knife and cut into the cake, putting a piece on the plate. "You'll be able to take this home," I said.

"Can you pass it around to the people who work here?" she asked.

"Sure," I said.

"I'll have a piece," Gloria said, waving both hands in the air.

"You don't need a piece," Miriam said.

"They could erect a statue to your sensitivity," Gloria said. "Happy birthday, darlin'," she said, looking at Tamara. Tamara's face softened and the lines that reached across her forehead faded to spindly creases. I don't think anyone had called her a term of endearment in ages. Gloria slid out of her booth and picked up her breakfast plate. "You know what? We are going to move over there with you because no one should eat alone on her birthday." Miriam sighed and followed. Gloria settled in and surveyed the table. "Now this is a birthday celebration," she said.

"Christine?" I turned to look at Tamara.

"I'm thirty-four."

"Happy birthday," I said, leaving them alone.

I worked my other tables that morning but kept my ear tuned to Tamara's party. Gloria and Miriam made her giggle and one time I swore I heard a belly laugh. Tamara delivered pieces of cake herself to the staff and any customer that wanted a piece. For a few minutes on that windy December day she felt normal again, whatever that meant, and she smiled. In a world where she heard emptiness as she walked the streets and sat alone in the park I believed she heard the song of people remembering her name. I watched her and realized that God was most likely felt in those ordinary moments — not in an explosion of light as I'd always thought or in the rumble of a storm but at the side of a child's bed reading stories, rummaging through a drawer for a bright scarf, or at a breakfast table with birthday cake and coffee.

TS never showed up at Betty's for breakfast or lunch. I reasoned that maybe he thought I was working at night now so he decided to come in during the dinner hours. I grabbed four empty produce boxes that Craig was throwing away and raced home to meet Zach and Haley as they got off the bus. My cell phone rang as I got out of the car. I didn't recognize the number but answered it anyway. "Christy?"

I set the boxes down and put my key in the front door, groaning. "What?"

"I want to see the kids on Friday," Brad said.

"As soon as your check arrives in the mail you can have your visits again."

"I am paying again." I didn't believe him. "And I'm coming on Friday."

"If that check is in my mailbox, you bet." I snapped my phone shut and ran to the mailbox. Maybe he was telling the truth. I pulled out a small stack of mail and flipped through it. Nothing. I shivered in the cold and ran up the driveway and kicked the boxes into the house, grabbing the phone off its cradle in the kitchen. I rummaged through the drawer with the phone book and found Patricia Addison's number. I dialed her cell and hoped she'd answer.

"Hello," she said.

I was so relieved to hear her voice. Although I'd only met Patricia once I had the feeling I could trust her. "Patricia, this is Christine." I realized she knew me by my given name. "*Angela* Christine Eisley. Angela's my first name but nobody calls me that. I go by Christine. I just didn't know when to tell you that when you were here." She laughed and I could hear children in the background. "Did I catch you at a bad time?"

"No, no," she said. "I just picked the kids up from school and we're headed home."

I looked at the clock and knew Zach and Haley would be running through the door any second. "I don't know if you can tell me this or not but my ex-husband is hammering me about visitation this weekend."

"Has he paid child support?"

"I haven't gotten a check," I said, watching the front window for the school bus. "But he says he's going to show up here on Friday. Do I have to let him take the kids?"

She paused. I wasn't sure if I was putting her in an awkward position. "What has your attorney told you in the past?" she asked, sidestepping the question.

"He's told me that when Brad pays child support he gets visitation."

"Have the laws changed since that time?" she asked.

I smiled. "I don't think so."

"No, they haven't."

"But what if he gets here and he rants and raves and threatens lawsuits and —"

"That's his choice," Patricia said. "You will have done nothing wrong." It's amazing how a word spoken in kindness or anger can set the course for the remainder of the day. Although I didn't know much more beyond Patricia's name, the grace in her voice and the choice of her words calmed me when I would ordinarily get up in arms after a call with Brad.

The school bus stopped in front of the house and the door swung open. I moved the boxes out of the entryway and set them on top of the kitchen counter. "Thank you, Patricia," I said, hanging up. The kids ran screaming up the driveway and fell inside the door, breathing hard. "Did you outrun Mrs. Meredith?" I asked.

Zach shook his head. "She wasn't at her

door today. Probably hanging upside down in the attic."

I took his coat from him and laid it on the back of the sofa. "How about something to eat before we go to Glory's Place?"

"I don't want to go there," Haley said, throwing her coat on the floor. "It's scary."

"You've never even been there," I said. I went to the kitchen and made each of them a peanut butter and jelly sandwich. "Each of you take your homework because you can do it there."

Zach took a bite of his sandwich. "Why do you work at night all the time?"

"I'm just doing it so we can have some extra money," I said.

"Why do we need extra?" Haley asked. "Don't we have like fifty dollars?"

I laughed. "Exactly! And we need more than that!"

Zach noticed the boxes on the kitchen counter. "What's in those?"

"Nothing yet but I'll need to pack our things in them." I didn't know how to tell them so I just came out with it. "We need to move to another house."

"Why?" Haley said. "I like this house."

"I like it, too, but I just can't afford it anymore. We need to find a place that's not as expensive."

"I don't want to move," Zach said.

I sat down beside him. "We have to move. It's not my decision."

His eyes filled with tears and he buried his face in my shoulder. "It's not fair," he said, rubbing his eyes on my shirt.

"We'll find a great place," I said, trying to convince him and myself.

I signed the kids up with a woman named Heddy Gregory at Glory's Place. She was a retired black woman with a tremendous smile and short-cropped salt-and-pepper hair. Her husband Dalton showed Zach and Haley where they could hang up their coats and gave them a tour of the center. I watched them out of the corner of my eye and could tell they were afraid; Haley held on to Zachary's hand and he didn't shake her off. When they finished the tour Zach snuck up to my side and tapped me on the hip. I looked down and he pointed to the basketball hoop. "You can go over there," I said. He tugged on my arm. "I need to fill out this paperwork but you and Haley can go play."

"It's all right," Dalton said, crouching down in front of them. "Everybody feels scared their first time here but as soon as you throw a basketball all that goes away this fast," he said, banging his hands together and pretending to scatter magical dust in front of him. He held his hand out and Haley grabbed hold of it.

"Wait a second," I said, bending over for a kiss. "Who are you?" I asked Haley.

"Mommy's angel," she said. I kissed her and leaned toward Zach.

"Do I have to say it?" he asked, whispering.

I smiled. "No, but you do need to let me kiss you." He leaned the top of his head toward me and I kissed it. They walked with Dalton to the basketball hoop and joined four other children who were already shooting baskets.

"They'll be okay," Heddy said, watching me.

I signed the forms and jumped in the car, crying as I pulled out of the driveway. I would have given anything to have some sort of normal schedule with my kids, to have more energy during the times we were together, and not be so consumed with the reality of bills, finding an apartment, and battles with their father. By the time I got off work tonight, picked them up, and got them home it'd be close to nine; too late for children to go to bed on a school night. I hated it but didn't know a way around it. I pulled into the back lot, wiped my face, and walked through the kitchen. "Cutie out there waiting," Betty said, laying the top crust over a berry pie. I hung up my coat and turned the corner to see TS leaving.

"Hey!" A table of customers turned to look at me and I realized how loud I was.

He turned and smiled. "I was supposed to be somewhere ten minutes ago," he said, holding the door open. "Did you check your coffee schedule?"

"I get a thirty-minute dinner break at seven o'clock Thursday night."

"I'll be here," he said, running out the door. Snow tumbled to the ground outside the window and he smiled as he passed it. My thoughts were as inconsistent as those flakes: *He's so handsome. What's the point? Maybe he'll love kids. When he hears about the kids he'll be gone. He's too young for me. I'm too old for him.* I felt silly for hoping but something somewhere, maybe in those flakes falling just beyond the window, or a voice inside, seemed to whisper, "You're still here. I'm still here." And something in me believed it.

Jason pulled a box out of the trunk of Marshall's car and carried it up the steps of Glory's Place. "Hey, what's that?" a small boy asked. "Can I help?"

"Sure," Jason said. "What's your name?"

"Zach. This is my first day," he said, following Jason back to the car.

"It's my first day, too," Jason said. Zach wrapped his arms around one end of the box and held it close to him. Jason backed slowly up the stairs so Zach could keep up. They set the box inside the door and Jason raised his hand in the air. Zach gave him a high five and ran off to play. Dalton and another volunteer were shooting hoops with a group of children while another volunteer sat at a table playing Sorry with three girls and opened cans of Play-Doh for two other children. A few girls and one boy pretended to cook in the kitchen and took each other's "orders." Some children worked on puzzles, others flipped through books, and a group of boys built towers with LEGOs. The room was full and loud but bearable.

"So you're Jason?" Heddy said. "Marshall's told us all about you."

"I'm not as bad as he makes me sound," Jason said, taking off his coat.

"He makes you sound like a superhero," Heddy said.

"Really?" Jason said. It didn't sound like his grandfather.

"Frankly, I haven't believed much of it at

all," she said, winking at him.

"These are the donations from the store for your Christmas boxes."

"We've been expecting those. I don't know what we'd do without your grandfather's donations of socks, underwear, hats, and gloves every year!" She walked in front of him and led him to the far side of the room where a large cubicle and cafeteria table was set up. "We need someone to help the kids with their homework. We send them over in groups of six. The older kids are good about sitting here and getting the work done but many of the younger children need supervision and help. Are you up for it?"

Jason would have rather played basketball but he nodded. "How long should they be here?"

"Until their work is done," Heddy said. She pointed to the pencils, erasers, and a pencil sharpener on the table. "I'll send the first six over while you sharpen the pencils." She opened a small white cabinet, pulling out a package of cookies and napkins. "They each get two cookies while they work. Gloria cringes because they're not homemade. She thinks children should eat cookies and milk while doing homework. Sometimes we have these. Sometimes we don't. It just depends on donations."

Four girls and two boys, one of them Marcus, bounded to the table carrying backpacks or loose papers with crumpled edges. Marcus came empty-handed but reached for a napkin. "I don't go to school so I don't have homework. I just come for the cookies," he said, holding his napkin in front of Jason. Jason laughed and set a cookie on it.

Three of the children busied themselves with math, English, and science books but Zach and Haley sat and watched. "Do you have any homework?" Jason asked.

Zach reached for his backpack. "Normally my mom helps me," he said.

"Is she working?" Jason asked. Zach nodded. "Well, I can help you today so when she picks you up it'll all be done. Is this your sister?"

Zach nodded. "She's Haley." Haley's legs stuck straight out over the edge of the chair.

"Hi, Haley," Jason said. "Do you have homework, too?"

"I have to do my letters and I hate letters," she said, throwing her backpack onto the table.

"She always whines," Zach said, pulling out a sheet filled with math problems.

"Can't I just eat a cookie like him?" she asked, looking at Marcus.

"Maybe these will help you like letters,"

Jason said, setting two chocolate cookies with vanilla centers in front of her.

Haley bit into one. "What's your name?"

"Jason."

"How old are you?" she asked.

"I'm twenty-four."

"Is that old?"

"It's older than you but no, it's not old."

"It sounds real old," Marcus said, waiting for another cookie.

"My mom's old like you." Haley said. "She's twenty-seven."

Jason laughed. "Better not say anything to her. Women don't like to be told they're old."

"She knows she's old. She always says, 'I'm getting too old for this,' when me or Zach do something bad."

Jason leaned over and read a math problem out loud for a first grader named Aiden. "The woman needed a dozen eggs but she only had eight. How many more did she need?"

"I know," Marcus said, raising his hand. "Forty-two."

Jason smiled and put his finger to his lips to quiet Marcus. Aiden put his pencil on his head and rolled it back and forth, thinking. "How many is in a dozen?" Jason asked. Aiden shrugged. "There's twelve in a dozen.

So if she has eight eggs how many more eggs does she need to make twelve?" Poor Aiden. He had no idea. Jason set out four cookies each on three napkins. "Okay. Here's twelve cookies. Can you find eight of them?" Aiden pointed to one plate of cookies and then a second. "So here's eight of the twelve. How many more cookies do you need to add to those eight to make twelve?" Aiden rolled the pencil up and down his forehead.

"I know!" Zach shouted at the end of the table.

"I know, too," a fifth grader named Demarius said.

Aiden looked up at Jason. "Four?" he said in a whisper.

"Exactly!" Jason said, putting the cookies back in the package.

He made his way to each of the children and then to the end of the table again where Haley stared at the letter *v.* "What is going on with *v?*" Jason asked.

"I hate *v,*" she said.

"She hates all the letters," Zach said.

"You could have had them done by now," Jason said.

"That's what Mom always says," Zach said.

Jason put his hand over Haley's and

helped her form a *v* on the page. "I don't like it here. It's scary," she said.

"She's always scared," Zach said. "It's not scary. There's no monsters or Bat Lady or anything."

"Are you scared?" Haley asked.

"I'm not scared of this place," Jason said. He sat down next to her. "But I am a little scared about something."

Her eyes were huge. "What?"

"I'm going out on a date Thursday. Well, kind of a date."

"With a pretty girl?"

"Not as pretty as you but she's close," he said. Haley smiled and attempted another *v* on her own. "So what do you guys want for Christmas?"

"A spaceship!" Marcus shouted.

"I want a pair of fairy wings so I can fly," Haley said.

"I want a star command building set," Zach said, "and a LEGOs kit that I can build an airplane out of."

"Cool," Jason said, watching Haley make a *v*. "What are you getting your mom?"

"She always says she wants us to make her something," Zach said. "So I'm going to draw her a picture and Haley won't do anything."

"That's because I need help and I can't

have Mom help me make something for herself," she said, slapping her pencil down on the table.

"Then make her the noodle thing again," Zach said.

"I don't want to make her the noodle thing again," she said, upset. "I want to make her something new but I can't." She turned away from her brother and put her head on the table.

"I can help you make something," Jason said. "What do you want to do?"

She lifted her head off the table. "I want to *make* her something." She picked up the pencil and erased a *v* that looked like a *u.*

Jason thought for a moment and popped a cookie in his mouth. "You know what? I work at a store that sells these clocks that children have to paint. Would your mom like that?"

"Yes!" Haley said, waving her pencil in the air.

Jason spent the rest of his time helping children with their homework and then shooting hoops with Marcus. He never noticed when Zach and Haley's mother picked them up.

EIGHT

Jason gathered the day's mail from the mail-room and closed the door behind him. The sound of a vacuum came from the stairs and he took them by two until he found a woman vacuuming up white powder. "What happened?" he asked.

"My cart started to fall," the woman said, turning the vacuum off. She was petite and thin with short thick curly hair that covered her head like a shower cap. "This container of cleaner fell and busted open. Poof," she said. "Everywhere."

Jason lifted the broom and dustpan from her cart and helped sweep the powder off the landing. "Are you the head of the janitorial staff?" he asked.

"Yes," she said. "And you're the owner's grandson."

"Jason," he said. "What's your name?"

"Shirley Cohen." She turned the vacuum back on and ran the hose along the stairs.

"How long have you been here, Shirley?"

She talked over the machine. "Oh, boy," she said, using her fingers. "Eighteen years."

"Always cleaning?" He couldn't imagine the boredom.

"Marshall wanted to move me to one of the departments but the thought of standing there and dealing with people. Eh," she said, throwing her hand in the air. "I love to clean. Might as well do what I like."

Jason emptied the dustpan into the garbage can on her cart. "Have you ever wanted to work anywhere else?"

She finished the stairs and turned off the vacuum. "No," she said, pulling a tissue from her smock pocket. "Marshall's good to me. He's fair. I don't take advantage of him and he doesn't take advantage of me or my staff. He knows the names of my children and asks how they're doing. When you're young you want this, that, and the other in a job but after a while you want something more than that."

"And this is more?" Jason asked, sticking the dustpan back onto its hook.

She turned the vacuum back on and shouted over it. "It is for me!"

Jason ran down the stairs, leaping down the last three steps, and landed face to face with her . . . the irate black lady from the toy department! Her hair was bigger than before and this time she had a ribbon wrapped around it. She was wearing a bright red turtleneck, black slacks, and high-heeled boots that made her tower above his head. "H-h-h-ello," he said, stammering. "Remember me?"

"Yeah, I remember you," she said, flicking long, purple nails in his face. "Mr. I Love Christmas."

"I actually *do* love Christmas," he said, following her to Santa's workshop. She adjusted a lollipop on the walkway leading to the front door. "I am pro-Christmas." She picked up one of the giant lollipops and leaned it against her shoulder. "I may have come across as anti-Christmas but that would be wrong." He waited for her to say something. "And I'm sorry if I came across in any way other than 100 percent *for* Christmas."

She tapped the lollipop against her shoulder and pushed out her lips. "You're nothing like your grandfather, you know that?"

"I have been made aware of that, yes," he said, tucking the mail under his arm. She smiled and stuck the lollipop back into position. "So? Are we good then?"

"We're good, Christmas," she said, walking past him to a display of games.

"Well, you know my name's Christmas," he said, smiling. "But I don't know yours." He paused. "I offended you. The least I can do is learn your name."

"Lana," she said, straightening the display.

"That's beautiful," he said.

"I know it is. My father named me. He was a porter in a hotel on the weekends, and one weekend Miss Lana Turner herself rode up in the elevator with him and gave him a ten-dollar tip."

"Wow, things may not have turned out so well for you if Yo-Yo Ma slipped him a twenty." She threw her head back and cackled. "Of course kids probably wouldn't have teased you. They love to play with yo-yo's." She cackled again and he laughed out loud. Every time her hair bounced, the smell of jasmine wafted toward him. "I like you, Christmas."

"I knew you would," he said, searching the aisles for the clock box.

"What do you need, love?" He smiled. He'd gone from Christmas to love in about a minute.

"The clock that you paint."

She put a long-necked stuffed giraffe back into a bin as she walked past him. "We're out of the clocks. We have this heart box," she said, handing it to him.

"I really liked the clock," he said.

"For a girl or a boy?"

"Little girl painting it for her mother."

She whistled through her teeth. "She will be all over this box and her mother will love you for it."

"I'm not interested in her mother's love," Jason said, paying for the box. "I was just looking for something easy." He read the back of the box as he climbed the stairs and sighed. "What have I gotten myself into?"

He put the bag under Judy's desk and walked to the coffeemaker. "I'm ready to take that test again!" he said, yelling back to Marshall.

Marshall opened a file cabinet and pulled out a sheet of paper. He put on his glasses and wrote something on the back of the paper before handing it to Jason. "Feeling confident?"

Jason held the cup of coffee up as if toasting his grandfather. "I know every person's name in this building."

Marshall smiled and put the test in front of him. There weren't any questions regarding the history of the building but every one was a person's name. "Who are the two people who work in the mailroom?" "What are the names of the security guards?" "Who is the supervisor of toys and Santa's workshop?" On and on it went until Jason filled in the last blank, smiling as he wrote Shirley Cohen's name. "Give me my check," he said, waving the test in the air.

Marshall stepped down from his office, looked over the answers, and then over his glasses at Jason. "You did it."

"I told you I would." Jason sipped his coffee and held out his hand. "Check, please."

Marshall laughed and walked up to his office, pulling out two weeks worth of checks from a file drawer. "So how does it feel?"

"To get paid for work I've already done? Awesome!"

"To know everyone's name," Marshall said, sitting on a chair across from Judy's desk.

Jason folded the checks and put them in his back pocket. "I feel like I'm a vital part of humanity," he said.

Marshall rolled his eyes. "A point is lost on someone like you."

Jason grinned. "I get your point." He looked out the office windows into the store. "I know everyone's name and because I took the time to learn them I know about them as a person. Satisfied?"

"Perfect. Now what are you going to do with the rest of your life?" Jason's phone vibrated in his pocket and he pretended not to notice. "You're not on the sales floor. Go ahead and take it," Marshall said, closing his office door.

Jason pulled the phone out fast and flicked it open. "Hello," he said.

"Hey, babe," Ashley said. The hair on the back of Jason's neck stood on end. He'd forgotten all about her. "I've been driving a couple of hours already and should be there by two or so."

Judy sat at her desk wearing her red jingle bell sweatshirt. She looked great. "You know, I'm perfectly fine to come back."

"No, you're not," Marshall said.

"My doctor says yes but you say no. Let me see . . . who should I believe?"

Marshall paced back and forth in front of her. "You're avoiding the question."

She covered her face with her hands and moaned. "I am not avoiding it. I've already answered your question every way I know how. If you feel that you want to do this. Do it." She banged on the desk. "This is your desk. This is your store. This is your life. If you feel strongly about it —"

"What do you think Jason will do?"

She leaned back and screamed. "Just say what you want to say and don't worry about Jason."

"I can't call Linda and talk to her about it on the phone. It'd be better if she was here."

"Well, that's a few more days," Judy said. "If you want to wait and talk it through with Linda, wait."

He stopped and looked at her. "What would you do?"

She pushed her chair back and stood up. "You know what? You're right. I am not ready to come to back to this."

"I told you you weren't. Take a few days and enjoy the grandkids."

She slid gloves onto her hands and walked to the door. "I will."

He followed her, tapping her on the shoulder. "Seriously . . . should I wait for Linda?"

She threw her head back and laughed.

Glory's Place was closed on Thursdays so I spent Wednesday night and the drive into work Thursday morning calling sitters again. When the breakfast crowd left and my tables were cleaned I checked my phone to see if anyone had called back. I made another call and waved at Tamara when she sat at a booth. "Renee," I said, into the phone, "is there any chance you'd be available tonight to watch the kids? I promise I'll never bother you again."

"I can kind of do it," Renee said. "I have to drive friends to the airport this afternoon. I couldn't be at your house when the kids get off school but could be there by five thirty or so if that works."

It would have to work if I couldn't find anyone for the whole time. I carried the coffee to Tamara's table and she looked up at me. "Sitter troubles?" she said.

"If I had a dime for every minute I spent trying to find one."

"How many kids do you have?"

"A boy and a girl," I said.

"That's what I have," she said. "My boy's eleven and my little girl is nine."

"I didn't know you had children," I said. Really, I didn't know anything about her. "Coffee and a day-old?" She nodded and I crossed to the baker's rack to pick out a pastry. I threw it back into the basket and went to the register where I input a bowl of oatmeal instead. The oatmeal warmer was at the end of the cook's line and I lifted the lid, dipping out a bowl full. I put a small cup of berries covered with brown sugar onto the tray and delivered it to Tamara. She looked up at me. "Someone ordered it for takeout and never showed up." She didn't move. "Who orders oatmeal for takeout, right? Probably why they didn't come get it." She looked down at it. "If you don't eat it we'll have to throw it out."

"Really?"

"Hopefully it's still warm. I dumped it out of its to-go container. The fruit makes it really good."

"Thanks," she said, pouring the fruit and sugar concoction on top of the oatmeal. I took orders from a table of four and from a new couple who sat in the booth next to Tamara. I delivered their food and checked back with Tamara. The oatmeal was only halfway gone.

"You're a slow eater," I said.

"Just enjoying it," she said.

"Do you ever bring your children in with you?"

She stirred the oatmeal and lifted the spoon up and over. I knew I'd said something wrong. "They live with their dad." She took a bite and stared into the bowl.

"My kids live with me." She looked up at me. "How often do you get to see them?"

She wadded the napkin in her hands. "It's been over a year."

I was never good in these situations. I never knew the right thing to say. "Does he have sole custody?"

"He does now," she said, turning the oatmeal up and over, up and over.

"I've been divorced for four years and it's been a nightmare." She let out a puff of a laugh. "For you, too?"

She shook her head, wadding the napkin in her hand again. "I'm the nightmare in our divorce."

I glanced over my tables to make sure they had everything and that no one new had showed up. "What does that mean?"

"I taught third grade and my husband worked in computer sales. Still works in computer sales. I went to the thirtieth birthday party of a friend one night. Girls only, you know, and one of the ladies, a real snooty 'something's stuck up her butt' kind of lady with expensive clothes pulls out some meth and starts offering it around. We were all slightly buzzed because we'd had a lot of wine and she said we'd feel even better in a few minutes. I loved it. I'd never felt so charged in my life." She pulled up a spoonful of oatmeal and tilted the spoon so the oatmeal dripped back into the bowl. "I woke up in the bed of my friend's husband. Some birthday present I gave her. And I was hooked on meth. Your face says there's no way it could happen that fast. I didn't think so either but it does . . . and it did."

"So drugs were the reason you lost custody?" I asked, keeping my voice low.

"Drugs were one of the lesser charges," she said, pulling the toast apart. "I kept those hidden from my husband. He had no idea. All he knew was I had a lot more energy throughout the day. The problem was I lost my job halfway through the school year. I had a hard time showing up on time and had a tendency to leave early. You do that a few weeks in a row and people notice. Without my paycheck I had a harder time paying for the meth and before long we were late paying the mortgage and car loans and that pissed off my husband." She tried to take a bite and stopped.

"I'm sorry," I said. "I'll let you eat."

"No. It's okay. I've told this story a lot in treatment. It always ends the same. You'd think I'd know that by now." I caught Karen's eye and she raised her brows, looking at me. My tables were now empty and I found myself glad for the lack of work. "We separated but had joint custody of the kids. They came to my apartment one weekend and I went to the apartment manager's place after the kids had fallen asleep with the intention of screwing him for rent before I went back to my apartment. But he had some crack and some booze and before I knew it it was morning and my kids were gone. My daughter had woken up in the middle of the night and was terrified when she couldn't find me. She called my husband and he came to get them. He left twenty-seven messages on my answering machine through-out the night. When I woke up around lunchtime I ran up the flights of stairs to my apartment and threw up when I saw they were gone. The phone started to ring and I saw it was my husband. I picked it up and he called me a whore." Her voice caught and she turned to look out the window. "And I couldn't deny it."

A long and empty stretch of silence followed. I had no idea what to say. Winds blow us off course. I've been swept away myself by unexpected gusts but then there are storms of my own making and those have been more destructive and costly. This storm was Tamara's and the aftermath was devastating. There are days when it's hard for me to live inside myself because it's there that I'm most angry and hurt and the failure of my life beats the loudest. I looked at Tamara's small frame and blue-veined hands and wondered what it was like living inside herself. I couldn't imagine. She pressed the napkin to catch a tear on her cheek and looked me in the eyes for the first time. "Long story short . . . I ended up on the streets for seven months so I could support my habit. I lost consciousness after a man beat me when I wouldn't do something he'd asked and two hookers found me and took me to a hospital. I was out of it for days but I could hear a woman talking. I had no idea who she was or what time of day it was. All I could hear was this whispering that sounding like a prayer in my head. 'Help her. Open her eyes.' That's what I heard. When I finally came to I heard this whispering again and opened my eyes to see an overweight black nurse checking the monitor by my bed. I listened as closely as I could to her whispering and she was praying. For me. Rita has four children, seven grandchildren, and an adopted former meth addict-prostitute in her family. She convinced me to go to a treatment center, and when I got out she introduced me to someone at the women's rescue mission where I've been for seven months." I was stunned and knew that anything I said would sound trite and stupid. "I know," she said. "It's unimaginable that a mother could do those things."

"No," I said. "I mean —"

"It's all right," she said. "I still can't believe it myself." She took a few more bites of her oatmeal and I sat feeling awkward and stiff and not at all helpful. "We have to be out of the mission at eight each morning for work . . . or to look for work and then back by four for classes and dinner."

"So when you're not working what do you do during those hours of the day?"

She smiled. "I go to the library and read. I like to read the books I always read to my kids at night. It makes me feel close. I sit in the park and think and hope and pray . . . a lot. I go to that church on the square and sit in the sanctuary and pray some more. They did a food drive for two weeks before Thanksgiving and because I was already there I helped every day with that," she said, laughing. "I do a lot of walking around town." It sounded horrible to me. She looked at me and smiled. "It's not so bad. Rita says, 'One step forward each day is the way back to the land of the living.' So that's what I try to do."

"But why haven't you seen your children?" I asked. "If you've been through treatment and are making strides to get your life —"

She shook her head. "They don't want to see me."

"How do you know that?" She didn't answer. "Did they say that?" She shook her head. "They *do* want to see you."

Tears pooled in the corners of her eyes and she looked out the window. "No, they don't. They haven't taken my calls in months."

"Because they don't understand what's happening to you," I said. "They're confused. I know they'd want to see you." She shook her head. "You're their mother. They love you. They'd want to see that you're doing well and that you love them. They'll see that you've changed and that you're still the mother they remember." She shook her head back and forth hard in front of me. "Yes. They'd want to see you."

"No!" she said, yelling. Karen looked up at me from the waitress station and Tasha stopped sweeping the floor.

I slipped out of the booth. "I'm sorry," I said, whispering. "I'll let you finish." I walked to the kitchen and leaned up against the aprons, closing my eyes.

"Are you okay?" Karen asked.

"Yeah," I said.

"What happened back there?"

I reached for the right words. "Sad," I said. "Just so sad."

"Can you tell me later?" I nodded. "She left and you have a table."

Tamara had finished the oatmeal and toast and I rang up her check, pulling four dollars out of my apron pocket for the oatmeal. *Four dollars for a story,* I thought. "Help her," I whispered, remembering Rita. *Take her back to her kids.* My eyes filled at the thought of her not seeing her children. *Give them love for her.*

Gloria and Miriam met me in Betty's back parking lot a few minutes before three. Gloria stayed crouched in the seat as I drove through town and into Ashton Gardens to spy out her mystery man. "This is ridiculous," she said. "What if someone sees us?"

"No one will see us," Miriam said. "I've worn my super-secret magical crystal ring that will make us invisible when I turn it on my finger."

Daylight flooded over the grounds of white and they sparkled and shone and nearly blinded me as I wound through the property. Two squirrels chattered in front of the car and scurried up a tree. "No one seems to be here, which is only logical in twenty-degree weather," I said.

"I'm going to throw up," Gloria said.

I turned the car left and headed for the greenhouse. "Here's a car," I said. The greenhouse windows were foggy and their borders etched with ice crystals. "I'll have to get out to look in the windows."

"Do not do that!" Gloria said, whispering with force. "Do not get out of this car!"

"Run!" Miriam said. "Run while I hold her off."

I opened the door as Gloria yelled again and I pulled my coat tight around me as I ran for the greenhouse. The first window was too foggy to see through and the next two were blocked with sprawling plants and trees. No one was visible from the back windows and I crept to the end where the entrance was found. I could hear voices inside. A brick retaining wall curved along the end of the greenhouse and I stepped onto it, hoping I could see through the trees that filled the entrance. I could make out the shape of a man's back as I lifted myself onto my toes to see through the leaves of the trees. It was a couple and they were kissing. The man turned toward the door and my heart raced when I saw his face. TS took the hand of the woman and walked toward the entrance.

I jumped off the wall and ran along the back of the greenhouse, keeping low. I jerked open the car door and threw it into reverse. My face was hot and my breathing was heavy as I sped through the streets.

Jason held on to Ashley, longing for a love he couldn't get by his sexual prowess or wit but one he could only receive as a gift. He

held on to her hoping for more but knowing there was only less. He looked into her
face wishing for a smile that would catch
his breath at the sight of it. He watched her
eyes and listened to her voice, hoping, like
his grandfather, for a look or a sound that
would leave him breathless and humbled by
the beauty of it. He watched. He hoped. He
listened. But there was nothing.

I walked into the house and rehearsed a
hundred things I'd say to TS tonight at
seven but knew I'd never carry through with
any of them. My mother said I never stood
up for myself. Maybe she was right. I put a
pot of water on to boil and reached for the
package of hamburger in the fridge.
Thoughts flooded my mind as I put it into
a skillet to brown. Why would he do that?
Why would he do that to me *or* her? I
drained the grease from the meat and
reached for a can of cream of mushroom
soup and some sour cream. The phone rang
and I saw it was my mother. "Hi, Mom," I
said, stirring the soup and sour cream into
the hamburger.

"Hey, sweetness. How is everything?"

I shook my head. Somehow she had the
ability to call at the worst moments.
"Good," I said, lying. I just couldn't tell her

the story of being evicted or about TS right now.

She was quiet. "Really? Your voice sounds different."

"I'm just making something for the kids to eat before I head to work," I said, watching the water bubbling up.

"Are you working nights now?"

I ripped open a bag of noodles and poured them into the pot. "Just a few nights. Gives me extra money for Christmas."

"Who's watching the kids?"

I knew she'd ask that. I didn't dare tell her they'd be alone for more than an hour. "Renee, from Patterson's. Remember her?"

"I don't think so," she said. "How's everything else? Has Brad been calling?"

"Of course," I said. I really couldn't bring myself to talk. "Mom, can I call you back later because Zach and Haley should be running in any minute?"

"Okay," she said. "Hey," she added before hanging up, "I was thinking of coming a couple of days before Christmas if that works with you and the kids." I glanced at my kitchen and knew it looked like the rest of my house. It was not welcoming for guests. "Richard will be traveling but he could meet me there the day before Christmas if that's all right."

It wasn't but I was stuck. "Sure," I said.

"I'll bring a big turkey and make those cookies the kids like." She was quiet on the other end. "Christine, your voice really doesn't sound like you."

I laughed, trying to take her mind off it. "I assure you it's my voice, Mom. Maybe your ears are the problem."

"Okay," she said. "Love you."

"Faster, faster, faster," I heard Zach yell on the front porch. The key rattled in the door and I walked to it, turning the knob. "You can open your eyes now," Zach said, tumbling onto the floor. Haley took her hands from her eyes. "She was actually *standing on her porch* this time," he said.

"Mrs. Meredith?" I asked, taking his coat from him.

"The Bat Lady," Haley said, throwing her coat on the floor. "That was the closest ever."

"We could have been gone like that," Zach said, crashing his hands together and making the sound of an explosion.

"All right," I said. "Come into the kitchen. I want to give you your dinner before I leave for work."

"Not again," Zach said, heaving his backpack onto the sofa. "Who's watching us tonight?"

"Renee will be here again but she won't be here until five thirty. Look at the micro-wave. See, it says four o'clock. That means she'll be here in one hour and thirty min-utes. Wash your hands. You can eat and start your homework and by then she'll be here. Okay?"

I reached for two plates and filled them with noodles and stroganoff. "Okay, let's go over the rules again for being alone." We went through the list of do's-and-don'ts. "And I'll call a lot to make sure you're okay." I watched them eat at the table covered with unopened bills and the news-paper classifieds with apartments circled that I couldn't afford, and knew that mov-ing, mothering, and just making a way was my life for the next dozen years. *All part of the muck and marvel,* I thought, kissing the top of their heads. I didn't want to go. I wanted to stay and be with them in a way you want rainy days and warm blankets. They finished their dinner, I repeated the rules, kissed them again, and locked the door behind me.

It took a lot of strength to open the sliding glass door. The lock always stuck except on that afternoon. Haley turned it and slid open the door. Snow hung on the branches of the trees that lined the back of the duplexes and thin sheets of ice spotted the deck's surface. The argument sprouted up as they always did; one of the kids making an exaggerated effort to prove they're right. "Come back in!" Zach shouted from the door. "It's freezing in here now."

"No," Haley said, climbing up the deck railing. Her pink and purple princess nightgown wrapped around her knees in the breeze and she folded her arms to keep warm. "You said I can't fly."

"You can't!" Zach said, yelling through the small opening he'd left in the nearly closed door. "Only bugs and birds fly."

"I *can* fly," Haley said, swinging her leg to the top railing. "Last night I was flying over these trees. If I had wings I'd fly to the top of that high, high one."

"Wings are fake and people can't fly. You dreamed you were flying. Mom always tells you that." He opened the door a few inches wide. "Get down before we get in trouble."

She opened her arms and the wind took her breath. She took a small step forward and her foot slipped on the icy railing plunging her forward. Her shriek was piercing but short and then she was quiet. Zach shoved the door open and ran onto the deck, screaming her name. He ran down the steps. Her face was in the snow and one leg was bent beneath her. "Mom!" Zach yelled, touching his sister's back. "Haley! Mom!"

"Watch out, Zachary," the voice said. A hand pulled his shoulder back and he stepped aside. She knelt down in the snow and Zach screamed at the sight of her.

NINE

The clock ticked too slowly that afternoon and I dreaded every second of it. I was never good at confrontation and still had no idea what I would say to TS. *Kiss any beautiful girls lately? Have you ever been to Ashton Gardens . . . I hear it's a great place to make out.* At every thought I came up with nothing.

"So," Betty said, sidling up to me at five o'clock. "Tonight's the night."

"Not really," I said, refilling the saltshakers at my tables. "I saw him kissing another woman today."

She slapped her forehead in disgust. "You're kidding, right?"

"I'm not that funny," I said, wiping excess salt from the shaker before moving to the next table.

Lori and Ann were the night waitresses and I could see them eavesdropping. "What are you going to tell him?" Lori asked, looking up from her own salt and pepper work.

"I'm going to tell him I have two children and that will end it once and for all. It always does."

"I'd rip him a new one if I were you," Lori said.

Betty squeezed my shoulders from behind. "There are other fish in the sea."

"That's what they say," I said. "Sure is a stupid saying."

She laughed. "There are other handsome young men who would be delighted to know you and your children, too." She gave me another squeeze for good measure.

"Thanks," I said. "Doesn't help right now but maybe tomorrow."

"Yes," she said. "My words of wisdom get richer with each new day."

My phone buzzed in my apron pocket and I checked to see who was calling. I didn't recognize the number so slipped it back into my apron. Within seconds voice mail buzzed and I thought perhaps it was someone calling me back about an apartment. Two of my tables filled and I decided to check the message later. I filled eight water glasses and my phone rang again; it was the same number from before. What if I missed a place to live because I couldn't take the call? I couldn't risk that and stepped into the kitchen to answer the phone.

"Christine?" I didn't recognize the voice. "This is Dolly Meredith from next door." I groaned, wondering what sort of noise the kids had been making to warrant this call.

"Hi," I said, realizing she said her first name was Dolly. Of all the names to attach to this woman!

"I don't want to alarm you but I have taken Haley to the hospital."

Panic throbbed in my chest and I backed into the walk-in cooler where it was quieter. "What happened?" My mind raced in a thousand different directions.

"She jumped off the deck railing and struck her head on the ground." My ears suddenly became hot and my hands turned cold. "She lost consciousness but regained it just over a minute later. She seems fine but as a nurse I knew that because she lost consciousness she needed to get checked out as a precaution."

I was breathing a little easier but was still scared out of my wits. Did she just say she was a nurse? "Is she okay? Is she scared?" I asked.

"Well, I would say this is just one big adventure for her," Mrs. Meredith said.

"Hi, Mom!" Haley yelled in the back-ground.

I heard her voice and smiled. "I'm coming right over," I said. "I can be there in about ten minutes." I found Betty in her office and told her what happened.

"Go," she said, waving me away.

Haley and Zach were listening to each other's hearts with a stethoscope when I found them sitting in a patient room in the ER. "What is going on in here?" I asked, pushing the curtain aside.

"Mom!" Zach said. "My heart beats faster than Haley's. That means I'm a faster runner, right?"

I hugged Haley to me and she squirmed from my arms so she could press the stethoscope to my chest. "Thank you, Mrs. Meredith," I said.

"Call me Dolly, Christine," she said, getting up from her seat. I never would have pictured her as a Dolly.

"I really need to know what happened," I said, holding Haley's face so she would look at me. A huge bump the size of a goose egg protruded from the side of her head.

"I told her not to but she tried to fly off the deck," Zach said. "She went straight down like a rock and banged her head on the ground."

Dolly smiled. "I think that's pretty much

what happened," she said. "Within a minute or so she opened her eyes."

I kept holding Haley while she fumbled with the stethoscope. "I don't know what they would have done if you hadn't been home," I said to Dolly.

"I try to keep my eye on them," she said. "Especially if I can see they're home alone. I watch them get off the bus and there's been a few times I've tiptoed over to your place to make sure they've locked the door. You never know with sitters."

I looked at her, stunned. I had read her wrong from day one and felt so ashamed. "I try not to leave them alone," I said. "It's just that my job . . ."

"I know," she said, smiling. "I've seen your" — she mouthed the next words — "ex-husband from time to time. I don't think I care for him very much."

I laughed. "That makes two of us," I said. "I didn't know you were a nurse."

"I retired three years ago," she said. "I did it for twenty-eight years. I was going to retire earlier but when I lost my husband I thought it would help occupy my mind and it did. I worked two more years after he died and moved into the duplex. It's a nice, quiet place to live."

"I know my kids don't make it so quiet," I

said. "And I'm sorry."

"Well, sometimes it's just too quiet at my place," she said, pulling Haley's hair back in her hand and playing with it. "And they're not so loud. It's just us bats have such good ears."

Zach and Haley snapped their heads to look up at her. "I am soooo sorry," I said.

She laughed, squeezing Zach's face between her palms. "They're just kids with wonderful imaginations," she said. "I know I'm not really a bat. Am I?"

Zach's eyes bulged and he shook his head. I laughed out loud. "Well, we won't be bothering you much longer. We've been given our walking papers."

"What do you mean? Did Ed kick you out?"

"I haven't been able to keep up with the rent and although I've paid some money each month I haven't been able to pay the full amount for the last four months. I'm twelve-hundred dollars behind and I'll never catch up now."

The sound of a growl came from her throat. "I can't believe he did that. You won't find a cheaper place."

"I know," I said. "But I'm trying."

Jason pulled the front door of Betty's open

and stepped inside, looking around. He stood at the counter and watched the waitresses hustle from the kitchen to the waitress station and then to their tables. The sound of metal landing on the floor echoed from the kitchen and Jason saw Spence, an afternoon cook, nursing a burnt hand. Jason strained to see to the back of the kitchen and then glanced over the dining room again. He spun around when he heard the ice dispenser and Spence collecting ice in a towel. "Excuse me," Jason said. Spence looked over his shoulder. "I'm here to see Rosemary."

"She's not here," Spence said. "She worked this morning."

Jason leaned onto the counter to hear him better. "Is she coming back?"

Spence pushed the ice into his hand and gave Jason a look that said he was stupid. "Her work's done."

Jason walked through the dining room and peered around the back wall into Betty's office. It was empty. He pushed open the back door before Lori could rip him a new one.

It was after nine o'clock when we got home. As Dolly assumed, Haley was fine but the doctor said she did the right thing in bringing her in for evaluation. "No more flying off the railing," he said, lifting Haley off the exam table.

We piled into my bed together and I wrapped my arms around both of them. In the back of my mind I thought about the hospital bill. I had dropped our insurance coverage less than a year ago because I couldn't afford it on my own. The thought of that bill made me nauseous. "I'm too squished," Zach said.

"I need to squish you," I said. "What in the world are you trying to do to your mother? What would I do if something happened to you?" I squeezed them hard and they both made choking noises.

"Come on, Mom," Zach said.

I raised up on my arm and leaned over Zach to kiss him and then Haley. "Can I fly tonight?" she asked, looking sheepish at me.

"You can fly all over the world tonight," I said. "But in the morning you keep your feet on the ground. Promise?"

"Promise," she said, hugging my neck.

We all slept like babies.

We were slammed at Betty's the next morning. A crowd pressed itself up against the counter and baker's racks, waiting for seats. Gloria and Miriam sat at their table before the busboy had the chance to clean it.

Gloria was drumming her fingers on the table watching me as I walked to them with their tea and coffee. "So," she said. "You have a lot of explaining to do."

I set her coffee down in front of her. "About what?" I couldn't imagine what I had done.

"We felt awful about that terrible debacle in Ashton Gardens and we came to see how things went with TS last night and discovered you weren't here." I nodded. "Betty said you were in the hospital with your *little girl*, a child we didn't even know existed. So, first things first. How is your little lamb?"

"She's okay. She tried to fly off the deck railing and knocked herself out."

"I keep telling Gloria the same thing will happen to her," Miriam said.

Gloria shushed her. "Have you heard of Glory's Place?" she asked.

"Yes! My kids went there for the first time this week."

"*I'm* Glory," Gloria said. "You didn't know that because we didn't know you had children, and I didn't get the chance to ask you on the first day we met because Miriam made me stop asking you questions."

"I knew it'd come back to me eventually," Miriam said, sorting the mail.

Gloria leaned onto the table. "The only way a spot could have been made for you is if it came through me or Heddy but I don't recall your name."

"Angela Eisley?"

"That's it!" she said. "You're Angela?"

"It's my first name. Patricia Addison knew me by that name the first time we met."

She slapped the table. "Well, all of this could have been avoided had I known about your children. Again, all Miriam's fault but we'll try to make up for it." Miriam sighed and ripped open an envelope. "Will your children be at the center tonight?" I nodded. "Then I'll meet them."

"No, you won't," Miriam said. "You're doing that dinner with Ned and his wife about donations."

Gloria nodded, remembering. "Are you working tomorrow?"

"Yes."

"Who's watching the kids? The center closes at six on Saturdays."

"Uh . . ."

"Miriam and I will watch them. We owe it to you."

"You and who?" Miriam asked, looking up over a letter.

"You don't owe me anything, Gloria. Please don't feel bad about the greenhouse.

231

I'll find a sitter."

"Well, you could keep looking," Gloria said. "Just wandering around in circles until you get fallen arches or you could use us." I laughed and she smiled. "At some point you come to the conclusion that we're all here to help each other." She poured cream into her coffee and looked at me. "Miriam and I will be at the center tomorrow afternoon," Gloria said. "We'll take them home from there."

Miriam cleared her throat and pretended to read a letter. "TS just walked in," she whispered.

My heart sped; I didn't want to face him. "Just get it over with," Gloria said, winking at me.

I grabbed two empty cups at the waitress station. "Hi," he said. He was cautious today for some reason. Feeling guilty I assumed. "I came last night but they said you weren't working." I ignored him and carried the cups and a pot of coffee to my customers at table three.

Another table of two sat down behind me and I turned to greet them. "Do you have any menus?" the woman asked. "We're in a bit of a hurry." I stepped to the counter and reached for a couple of menus, handing them to the couple. I walked toward the waitress station.

"Wait!" TS said, following me through the waiting crowd. "Can we do coffee some other time?"

He seemed sincere enough but then again so did Brad at the beginning. "I can't do that," I said. "It'd get really crowded with your girlfriend."

Tamara pushed open the office door at Wilson's and stepped inside, waiting for Jason to get off the phone. "Can I help you?" he said.

"I was checking on an application I filled out a few weeks ago."

Her arms were like coat hangers holding up an oversized jacket. She wrapped them around her and quickly pushed back a strand of hair behind her ear. Jason knew Marshall would never be interested in someone like her. "It's on file, I'm sure," he said. "But we're not hiring right now."

She walked back to the door and turned to look at him. "You don't need any seasonal help at all?"

"We have everybody we need," he said. "If something changes we'll call you."

She reached for the handle and pulled the door toward her. "But how could you call me? You don't know my name."

Jason smiled. "I'm sorry," he said. "It's been one of those days. Come on in and let me find your application." He slid the chair to a file cabinet and opened the middle drawer. Marshall stepped into the office and smiled at Tamara. Jason threw the oversized file on Judy's desk. "Okay, what's your name?"

"Tamara Meachum," she said, smiling at Marshall.

"I'll find your application and flag it," Jason said. "If something opens we'll call you."

Marshall sat on the edge of the desk. "What are you looking for?"

"Anything, really," Tamara said.

Marshall took the application from Jason and pulled his glasses from his shirt pocket, reading. "You were a school-teacher?" he asked, looking at her over his glasses.

"I was. Yes." She folded her hands in front of her and shifted from foot to foot.

"The address you have listed." She stared at the desk and nodded, expecting him to dismiss her because he knew where she lived and could only have assumptions of what she'd done. "I've known Lou, Margaret, and that crew for years. Do you like it?"

She noticed that he was careful not to let Jason know where she lived. "I like it very much," she said.

"A spot in our mailroom is open," Marshall said. "Personally, I think you're overqualified. . . ." She smiled at the compliment.

"I didn't know about that," Jason said.

"Holly told me yesterday that she's been accepted to college and will start at the beginning of January. That means we'd need to train someone now." He read through the rest of the application. "I can only imagine that you're fulfilled in the classroom and not a mailroom but this could be a stepping-stone back." He rested the application in his lap and looked at her. "Maybe?"

"I hope so," she said, so quiet that Jason had to strain to hear her.

"Are you interested?" Marshall asked.

She laughed out loud. "Yes! I've been looking so long that I'd almost given up hope."

Marshall took off his glasses and slid them back into his shirt pocket. "Nah," he said. "To lose hope is to decide that it was all just a bunch of hooey. Hope is waiting, you know?" She looked at him. There was nothing remarkable about Marshall; actually, he was plain in every way but somehow his words ran along her ears and sat upon her skin. *How did he say it?* she wondered. *Hope is waiting.* Hope *is* waiting. Hope is *waiting.*

Any way she thought about it it made her smile inside. "Jason will get you started on your paperwork. For references you can just put Lou and Margaret down. I've hired others on their word over the years."

Jason dug through Judy's file cabinet for the papers and handed them and a pen to Tamara. He left her alone and stepped into Marshall's office, closing the door. "There are so many other qualified applicants in the file," he said, whispering. He didn't get it. The accounting firm he had worked for would never hire a woman like that.

"It's the mailroom. It's not rocket science," Marshall said. "She'll be fine,"

Jason put his hands on Marshall's desk and leaned toward him. "She's strung out on something."

Marshall sorted through his paperwork. "She was," he said. "No doubt about it. I don't expect her to stay long."

"Because she'll relapse?"

"Maybe. But I think she'll want her life back. Sooner than later, I hope."

Christmas was seven days away and I hadn't purchased one present. The kids would take the bus to Glory's Place after school so I decided to walk to Wilson's before my second shift started. I took the stairs to the first floor and walked the aisles of toys looking for the space command building set Zach wanted. It was on the bottom shelf and marked at $39.99. I looked around for something similar and cheaper but there wasn't anything. "Can I help you find anything?" An attractive black woman wearing a bright red scarf draped over a purple sweater with the name Lana pinned to it stood next to me.

"Do you know if this will go on sale?" I asked, holding the building set.

"That was on sale last week," she said.

I sighed. I was always a day late and a dollar short. "Well, that's the story of my life," I said.

"Let me have it," she said, taking the box from me. "I'll look it up in the computer and if you want it for the sale price I'll sell it to you for that."

"That would be great," I said, following her to the cash register. She scanned the bar code and I took off my coat. I realized I'd left my apron on and pushed my tips deep into the pockets.

"Twenty-eight ninety-nine," she said. "Do you want it?"

"Yes," I said. She held it for me while I looked around. A pair of flimsy pink wings hung on an endcap along with fairy wands and slippers. They were ten dollars and had Haley's name written all over them. I found the same heart box I'd seen the last time I was in Wilson's and picked it up. Haley would love to paint and decorate it but I knew I wouldn't have the time or patience. I set it down and picked up a tin can filled with four different card games. I set that in my basket for both of them along with the game of Monopoly Jr. on sale for eight dollars. Zach loved to put together model cars and planes so I bought him a shining red Corvette. A Barbie doll with a pink sparkling dress and flowing blond hair smiled at me from a box and I knew Haley would love her. She was on sale for $8.99. Zach had always wanted a football small enough for his hands and they had one in the colors of his favorite football team so I threw it in my basket.

"Are you finding everything today?"

I glanced up to see an older man smiling at me. "Yes," I said, feeling awkward in my work apron. The princess dress up game Haley wanted was on the bottom shelf and I looked at the price. Way too much right now. I found princess dress up shoes and a princess coloring book with sparkling Magic Markers. A small stuffed dog with his head sticking out of a pretty pink purse was on sale for ten dollars along with a LEGOs construction set. I looked over the things in my basket and couldn't wait to wrap them. The kids would flip! I made my way toward the cash register when my phone rang. I stopped and pulled it out of my apron pocket. The word *private* appeared on the screen and I thought it might be someone calling back from my apartment search. "Hello." The connection was terrible. It sounded like the person asked for Hillary. "This is Christine," I said. "Christine," I said louder. I noticed the older man looking at me from the stairs and I stepped back into the aisle so I wouldn't be so noisy.

"Christy!" My blood ran hot.

"What?" I whispered hotly.

"I can't come for the kids after all today."

"Oh, really! Because your check never showed?"

"No, because something came up. The check's coming. It'll be there tomorrow. Listen —" I hung up the phone and walked to the cashier.

I couldn't believe I had as much as I did for less than a hundred dollars. The sale-slady wished me a merry Christmas and handed me two sacks that I carried through the store and out onto the sidewalk.

Marshall stopped when he got to the office door and ran back down the stairs to the toy department. He scanned the floor. "Did that young woman leave?" he asked.

Lana turned to him. "The one who was just here?"

He nodded. "Did she leave?" Lana nodded. "Was she a waitress?"

"I have no idea."

"Did you see her wearing an apron around her waist?"

Lana shook her head. "I didn't notice. Why?"

He opened the cash register. "Did she use a credit card?"

Lana closed the drawer. "She paid cash."

"She said her name was Christine, right? That's long for Christy."

"I didn't ask her her name!"

Marshall laughed. "I always knew I could be a private investigator and now I've proven it!" He ran up the stairs and through the main aisle to the front door. All the parking spaces were full. No one was about to back up onto the street. He darted around the back of the building to watch cars in the parking lot. A woman with three children was getting out of a minivan and a man was driving away in a black sedan. "Missed her," Marshall said. "But she's out there."

Jason pulled the heart box out of the bag and held it in front of Haley. "How about that for your mom?"

"Oh, yeah!" she said, clapping her hands together. "She'll love it."

"All right," he said. "Let me help with everyone's homework and when I'm done we'll start this. Okay?" She jumped up and down. "But you need to do your letters." She started to say something. "No whining. We can't do the box if your letters aren't done." She ran for her backpack.

Aiden plopped his backpack onto the table and pulled out a folder with a sheet of sentences. "I can't read these," he said, pushing his palm into his forehead.

"Sure you can," Jason said. He helped the other children at the table get situated with pencils and erasers and made sure all their homework was out before he sat next to Aiden. He covered up two letters in a word and held his index finger under the first letter, an *h.* "What letter is this?"

"*H,*" Aiden groaned.

"What sound does it make?"

"Ha," Aiden said.

Jason uncovered the next letter. "What's that?"

"A," Aiden said.

"That starts all the letters," Marcus said, interrupting.

"What sound does it make?" Jason asked Aiden.

"Ay," Aiden said.

"What else? That's the long sound. What's the short sound?" Aiden stared up at him. *"Aa.* Like *at* or *apple.* Put the *h* and the *a* together with that short *a* sound now." Aiden sounded out the two letters and Jason uncovered the *t.* "Now put the *t* on the end. Put it all together."

"Ha-t," Aiden said. "Hat."

"So if that's hat," Jason said. "What is this word?" he asked, pointing to *s-a-t.* Aiden stared at the paper. "The only new letter is an *s.* What does that say?"

"S-s-at," Aiden said.

Marcus grabbed another cookie and looked up at him. "Are you a teacher?"

Jason laughed. "No."

"You should be," Aiden said. "I like you better than Miss Albrecht."

Jason made his way from one child to the next and was surprised how at ease he felt. When the kids finished their work Jason double-checked it for errors and helped Aiden clean up gray, smoky eraser marks from his paper. Haley sat down with the second group of kids and showed her finished letters to Jason. He smiled and she pulled out the heart box to begin work.

"Okay," Jason said. "It says to paint it first. Do you know your mom's favorite color?"

"Purple," she said, reaching for the small tub of paint.

She splattered the paint on in great runny gobs and Zach shook his head. "That's too messy," he said, watching her.

Jason showed her how to use the brush to even out the paint and held it in front of her so she could paint the sides. Zach and the other children finished their homework and ran off to play, leaving Jason and Haley alone. "Okay," he said. "We can paint some of her favorite things on the sides. Does she like a certain flower or bug or anything?"

Haley lifted her shoulders and squinched up her face. "Beats me," she said.

"All right," he said, thinking. He remembered the conversation with Rosemary and said, "How about a hydrangea?"

"What's that?"

"It's a flower," he said, dabbing the brush to look like clusters of petals. "When I think of hydrangeas I think of my grandmother. I bet your mom will love them, too." He finished a cluster of pink hydrangeas and turned to Haley. "I'm thinking bugs," he said.

"Why would she like bugs?" Haley asked.

"Not a bug like a dung beetle. A pretty bug. How about a butterfly?"

"I like them!" she said, smiling.

Jason outlined a small butterfly next to the flower. "I'm going to let you paint this. Okay, let's go to the other side. What over here? A kite maybe?"

"Sure," Haley said.

He outlined a perfect diamond-shaped kite with a long tail that swept over the side of the box. "And on top we'll glue all the jewels and glassy beads. How's that sound?"

Haley began to paint the green stem of the flower and smiled at her work. "Mom is going to hug me so tight for this. She was mad at me this week because I did something bad."

"What'd you do?" he asked, watching her.

"I jumped off the deck so I could fly and went to the hospital. I got knocked out but Zach said it's good my head is hard."

Jason laughed. "I doubt your mom is mad at you for that. She's probably pretty grateful that you're okay."

Haley stuck her paintbrush in a cup of

water and swished it around. When it was clean she wiped it on a paper towel and stuck it in the red paint, making thin lines on the butterfly's wings. "How was your date?"

"How'd you know . . . oh, yeah, we talked about that, didn't we?" She nodded, keeping her eyes on the butterfly. "Not so good. We never got to go out and then she got really mad at me."

"Why?"

"She thinks something is true but it isn't."

"Why can't you just tell her the true thing? My mom always says if we tell her the truth that we won't get into as much trouble."

He laughed and held the box steady for her. "Well, she's pretty hot right now. I need to let her cool down."

"I can be your half girlfriend until she's ready."

"Deal!" he said.

Most of my tables were clean and prepped for breakfast at eight thirty that night. I had two tables of customers left but Lori said she'd take care of them for me so I could pick up the kids. I grabbed my coat off the back wall in the kitchen and turned in my tips to Spence who gave me big bills for them. Between the tips at breakfast and din-

ner I had made almost one hundred dollars. "Not bad," Spence said. "Good Christmas shopping money."

"Got it all done today," I said, slipping
the money into my wallet. "See you tomorrow." I pushed open the back door and the
wind caught my breath. Holding my purse
to my chest I ran across the parking lot for
the car. I reached for the handle when
something caught my eye. I stepped to the
rear of the car; the trunk was open. I lifted
it and gasped. Everything was gone.

TEN

I spun in every direction. I'm not sure what I was hoping I'd see: a woman about to put the sacks into her car or a man walking across the lot saying, "Oops, I accidentally took these out of your trunk." The trunk hadn't been pried open; there weren't any scratches or gouges. Somehow I hadn't closed it all the way and I knew it. I sat in the car and cried for what I'd done and lost and the reality of how all you get for pain is more pain.

I called when I got to Glory's Place and told them I was too sick to come inside for the kids; in truth, I was. They sent Zach and Haley out to me and I half-listened as they told me about their night.

"Is something wrong, Mom?" Haley asked after she brushed her teeth. I shook my head and held the blankets up so she could crawl into bed.

"Can you read?" Zach asked.

"It's too late," I said. "Let's make up for it tomorrow." He didn't argue but lay down. I sat on the edge of his bed.

"What is Christmas, Zach?"

He furrowed his brows and screwed up his face. "Huh?"

"What is it to you?"

"It's Jesus' birthday," he said.

"So why do we give gifts?"

"You said it was because God gave Jesus to us as a gift of love so we give gifts to say we love people."

I was beat and couldn't smile. "What if there weren't any presents? Would you still know how much I love you?" Tears were in my eyes and I concentrated hard so they wouldn't fall.

He lifted himself up and wrapped his arms around my neck, squeezing it. "It's okay, Mom," he said. "We have a lot of stuff." I reached for the light beside his bed before I started to cry and kissed his forehead. I couldn't speak.

The lights from the Christmas tree filled the living room with a soft half-light and I noticed the letter under the tree. I grabbed it and pulled it from the envelope. *God, help me,* it said. I was so weary of plodding my way through life. It seemed that I'd just come up for air when something else pulled me down. I ripped up the letter, shoved it back inside the envelope, and lay down on the sofa. The vision of someone taking the kids' toys raced through my mind. Some people would have closed the trunk in an act of kindness but not this jerk. He or she saw two bags of gifts and didn't look to see what they were; it didn't matter. I didn't matter. My kids didn't matter. Sleep wouldn't come for hours.

Marshall and Jason pulled into Glory's Place a little after nine. The call for volunteers had gone out a few days before: help was needed to box the donations and deliver them to families. A small assembly line had been created on the far end of the building, away from the basketball court and activities. Dalton and Heddy were leading this first group of volunteers that included Marshall. "I always know Christmas is close when you come in to volunteer," Dalton said.

Marshall smiled. He and Dalton had been doing this together for years. "Where's Gloria?" Marshall asked.

"She and Miriam are second string today," Dalton said. He moved next to Marshall and looked over the list on his clipboard. "You look tired, Marshall."

"Ah, just this season. I'm getting tired of working through Christmas. Linda went away to visit the kids and that worked for a long time but now I'm just tired of it."

Dalton patted him on the back. "You've got an anniversary coming up, right?"

"He can remember yours but ours slips by him," Heddy said, shaking her head.

"I was a day late!" Dalton said, yelling over his shoulder. He looked at Marshall. "Maybe that'd be a good time to make some changes."

"He'll help you change but forty years later I still can't get him to pick up his socks," Heddy said.

"It takes a while to form a habit," Dalton said, winking at Marshall. "All right," he said, banging his hand against the clipboard. "Let's load these boxes and stack them against the wall."

Someone put in a bottle of shampoo and moved the box to the next person who placed a tube of toothpaste and two toothbrushes. The box made its way down the table and each person put in deodorant, rice, canned beans and corn, cereal, peanut butter, crackers, flour, sugar, hats, gloves, socks, and shoes: one child's pair and one adult's pair according to the sizes written on the side of the box. Several boxes contained two small toys for younger children. One day Gloria hoped to provide more for each family but she relied solely on donations and each year they were able to give a little more than the year before. Families would pick up the boxes between now and Christmas and whatever boxes were left would be hand delivered.

Jason stacked the last of the boxes and stepped into Gloria's office to call his headhunter about a job. The call came late yesterday as Jason was finishing at Wilson's. "The firm's well established," Louis said. "They've been in business since 1948. They have an expanding client list and need more accountants. You fit their profile to a T." The money was great and the job started January 2. Jason dialed Louis on his cell phone. The interview was set for Tuesday afternoon.

"Where are you going for Christmas?" Haley asked, dropping a black chip into a slot of Connect Four.

"I don't really know," Jason said, dropping in a red chip. "I'm going to have a job interview right before Christmas so I might just hang out and stay with my friends."

"Boring," Haley said, dropping in another black chip. She wasn't even close to getting four in a row. "Are you going to move away?"

Jason dropped in another chip. He could have won a few turns ago but kept the game alive for her sake. "Maybe. I need to find a job in accounting. That's what I do."

She shook her head. "No, you don't. You help kids."

No one had ever described him as someone who helped kids. "I'm just doing this through Christmas."

"Then you won't help kids anymore?"

"This really isn't my thing. I'm good at accounting," he said, dropping in a chip away from hers so she could win.

"No, you're not."

"Do you even know what accounting is?"

"Nope," she said, dropping in a black chip to win. "But I know you're good helping kids."

He cleaned up the game and ignored what she said.

I wasn't in the mood for little Lovey Love or his indulgent mother today. His rounded, diapered butt ran at least ten laps from the display case to the table and back and he never listened when his mother asked him to "Sit down, Lovey Love." I stepped around him a dozen times and exchanged glances with Karen. When Lovey Love reached for my tray and sent the dirty dishes stacked on it clanging to the floor I'd had enough. I knelt in front of him as I cleaned up the broken pieces and said through my teeth, "Get in your seat and *stay* in your seat." His eyes grew round and large as he backed up to a chair and sat down.

"It's all right, Christine," Betty said. "We'll get it. Take a break." I walked to the kitchen and pressed a tissue to my eyes.

"What's up?" Betty was behind me but I couldn't face her. I had disrespected a customer and this wasn't going to go well. "You've got Lovey Love trembling in his diaper. All this time no one knew how to get Lovey Love's little butt in a seat and you took care of it with one tray of broken dishes."

I laughed out loud and dried my eyes. "I'm sorry, Betty."

"His mother should be sorry but she hasn't said a word. What's happening?"

"Just a really bad night. My car was broken into."

I didn't tell Betty what was taken; I never got the chance. Her hands were waving around her head as she marched to her office, "Did you hear that, Craig?" Craig flipped a row of French toast and craned his neck to hear her. "I'm going to call about getting some more lights in that lot. No! A security man. That's what I need!" She flopped the phone book on top of her desk. "Craig! How do I find one of those security men?" Craig listened to her babble and finally looked at me. I shrugged and walked back to my tables.

Lovey Love and his mother were gone but TS was at their table. He was handsome and charming but I couldn't take it today. "Listen," he said, standing as I approached the table. "I'm not that guy that you think I am." I tried to step back but he grabbed my arm. "Ashley and I dated some in college." She had a lovely name and a beautiful face to go with it. "We've tried to make it work out of college but it doesn't. She came here and I told her it was over. We weren't even dating anymore."

I pulled away and walked past him to the waitress station to fill five glasses with water. "So she was just some crazy who *thought* she was dating you so she made a trip out of her way to come here and kiss you?"

He leaned close to me. "I know it sounds ridiculous but yes. There's nothing there and you have to believe me."

"Why should I believe you? I don't even know you. And you don't know me."

He grabbed my arm and turned me to face him. I could sense Karen eavesdropping. "But I want to know you. If I didn't want to know you would I eat the driest boiled egg in the history of the world?" That made me smile. "Would I eat here time and again if I didn't want to know you? Would I send a woman packing who wanted to kiss me? I know I could kiss her but I don't want to. I want to kiss you if you'd ever let me." He loosened his grip and looked at me. "Someone asked me if there was anything that left me breathless and humbled at the beauty of it. Up until two weeks ago I would have said no. But I can't say that anymore." I couldn't breathe. Words flew through my mind but none of them came out. "Can I please take you out for coffee?"

"Okay," I said, aware that both Karen and Betty were listening. "The restaurant is rented out Monday night for a Christmas party and I'm not working it. Do you want to meet somewhere or pick me up?"

He scrambled for a napkin on the table. "I want to pick you up." I gave him my pen and he wrote down my address. "Six o'clock?"

I nodded and watched him walk out the door. "Don't blow this," I said to myself or him or God or maybe all three.

■ ■ ■ ■

Marshall knocked on the door and waited. He knocked louder this time and heard shuffling inside the home. Judy opened the door and sighed. "It figures. I just popped in *An Affair to Remember* and was comfortable on the couch."

"I was in the neighborhood," he said. "I tried calling all day but you never answered."

"Because this was supposed to be the day of Judy. Dave said I could do anything I wanted so I thought I'd do crosswords and watch movies. So far I've done laundry, made breakfast and lunch, cleaned the bathrooms, watched twenty seconds of the opening credits of my movie, and stood here and talked to you."

"So this is a good time?" he asked, smiling.

"So much for the day of Judy," she said, letting him in. "So?" He sat at the kitchen table and shrugged his shoulders. She opened a cabinet. "You didn't have your talk, did you?"

He shook his head. "Jason's got a job interview. It'll pay an obscene amount of money and starts in January." She sat on the other side of the table and put a cup of coffee in front of him. "Why didn't you talk?"

"Aren't you too old to be babysitters?" Haley said as they got out of the car.

Miriam slapped her hands together. "That's exactly what I said."

Zach and Haley waved at Mrs. Meredith standing in her doorway and Gloria threw up her hand. "Who's that?"

"That used to be the Bat Lady," Haley said. "But now she's Dolly."

"Well, this is already more fun than Miriam and I would have at our homes," Gloria said, unlocking the door. "We don't have a Bat Lady next to us."

"I wouldn't rule out Mrs. Hirsch," Miriam said.

Gloria helped Zach and Haley take off their coats. "Your mom has told us so much about you."

"She's never told us about you," Zach said.

"And why would she?" Miriam said. "There are thousands of things more interesting than us. Like this beautiful Christmas tree."

"We did that!" Haley said, running for the tree. "See the snow I put on it!"

Miriam picked up a cotton ball from the table. "Oh, this is a truly spectacular idea," she said, gathering the cotton balls in her hand. "Why don't we stretch each of these balls so the cotton spreads out and drape it over each limb?"

"That'll look like snow laying on the branches!" Zach said, plucking a cotton ball from the table.

"And I can put my mom's present under it," Haley said, running for the heart box.

"Oh, how beautiful!" Gloria said, kneeling down in front of Haley. "Where did you buy this?" she asked, winking at Miriam.

"I didn't buy it. I made it. Me and Jason did it together."

"Jason?" Gloria said. "Oh, Marshall's grandson. I haven't met him yet. What do you think of him?"

"He's the best ever," Haley said.

"Well, I can't wait to meet him," Miriam said. "I've met the best for a day."

"I've met the best for a month," Gloria said. "But never the best ever." She held the box in her hands. "Would you like help wrapping this?" Haley nodded. "We'll get to this first thing after dinner." She stood up and looked at Miriam. "I'm going to start dinner," she said. She carried a bag of groceries into the kitchen. "Why don't you

258

get busy cleaning the bathroom?"

Miriam pushed her hair behind her ear. "Why is that every time we do this sort of thing that I am relegated to the bathrooms as you enjoy the comforts of the kitchen?"

"Do you cook?" Gloria asked.

Miriam studied her nails. "I don't see how that's relevant to my question."

"Do you cook?" Gloria asked again.

Miriam sighed and trudged to the bathroom.

Gloria opened the oven door and reached for the chicken and rice casserole when the doorbell rang. "Miriam, can you get that?" she yelled, pulling the casserole toward her. "My head's in the oven." The bell rang again.

Miriam left the bright yellow latex gloves on and turned the lock, opening the door. A man in a leather jacket stood on the porch. "Yes," she said.

"I'm here to pick up Zach and Haley."

The children were in Zach's room playing and Miriam stepped out onto the porch. "Their mother never mentioned someone picking them up. Who are you?"

"I am their father. I was supposed to be here yesterday but something came up. Who are you?"

Miriam bristled at his tone. "Christine never said you would be taking the children. You'll need to wait here while I call her." Gloria appeared in the doorway, listening.

Brad moved toward Miriam. "There's no need to call her. She knows this is my visitation."

"What's going on?" Gloria asked.

"This man claims to be the children's father —"

"I *am* their father!"

Miriam continued. "He's saying he has visitation."

"I'll call Christine," Gloria said.

"You don't need to call her," Brad said, trying to push past Miriam.

"If you take one step closer to this door I will rain fire down on your head," Miriam said, waving a yellow finger in his face. "Back off right now." Brad took a step back and stared at her. "We know all about visitation rights in this state so you better be sure you have those privileges tonight because if you don't we will make life very difficult for you. Go call," she said, looking at Gloria.

"Yeah, you tell her I'm not putting up with this shit anymore and am going to drag her ass back into court."

"I will say nothing of the sort," Gloria said, squaring off to him. "That's what lawyers and the court system are for. I can't believe you would use that kind of language when referring to the mother of your children! When you do call your lawyers you better be sure you have all your ducks in a row because I plan to call a meeting with Judge Reddy over this. If you're the father of these children you should act like it instead of like a fool."

"Go call her," Miriam said.

"I'll call her myself," Brad said, slinking away.

They watched as he backed out of the driveway, squealing the tires as he barreled down the street. "You'll rain fire down on his head?" Gloria said. "What exactly does that mean?"

Miriam folded her hands and brought the bright yellow gloves up under her chin. "And who exactly is *Judge Reddy?*"

They laughed and Gloria closed the door behind them. "How's your blood pressure?"

"High," Miriam said, fanning herself.

Gloria used the dish towel to fan her face. "I'm hot. It's like someone rained fire down on my head."

Miriam rolled her eyes and headed back to the bathroom.

Tamara sat in my section late in the afternoon, and I noticed she looked like she was in a hurry for me to get to her. "I haven't seen you in the last few days," I said.

Her eyes were wide and bright. "I got a job."

"Congratulations!" I leaned down and hugged her. "Where?"

"At Wilson's. In the mailroom. I already started."

I sat across from her. "Are you going to like it?"

"I think so," she said. "Mr. Wilson is really nice. He hired me. His grandson had said no but then Mr. Wilson came in and hired me right on the spot."

"So what does this mean?" I asked. "Will you still be part of the rescue mission?"

"I can stay in the program for another five months," she said. "Now that I have a job I can save for a place of my own."

"But what about your kids?" I watched her face but she turned to look out the window. "Will you see them for Christmas?" She shook her head. "Why not?"

"I have this job now."

"Tamara," I said, leaning onto the table. "Do you want to see them?"

A tear made its way down her cheek but she made no attempt to brush it away. She nodded. "But I can't."

■ ■ ■ ■

Gloria picked the casserole dish and the bowl of beans off the table. "Are you sure you have full bellies?" she asked.

"Full to the top," Haley said. "You should enter a pie contest except it'd be for chicken and rice."

"A chicken and rice pie contest!" Gloria said.

"You'd win!" Haley shouted.

"But if you're full to the top," Gloria said, "that means you don't have any room for a chocolate chip cookie."

"Yes, I do," Haley said. "There's room down here in my leg."

"Both of my legs are empty," Zach said.

Gloria laughed and set the plate in front of the children.

"Yesterday was our last day of school," Zach said.

"I know!" Gloria said. Then it dawned on her. "Does your mother have a sitter for you on the days that the center is closed?"

Zach shrugged. "Sometimes we watch ourselves," he said.

Gloria glanced at Miriam. "Do you ever go with your father?"

"He says he doesn't have money to pay

my mom to help with us so we don't see him much."

"Only when he can pay," Haley said. "But he can't do that right now because he got a new motorcycle."

Miriam rolled her eyes. "Do you like to see him?"

Haley shrugged. "I don't like his apartment. He doesn't have toys or much food and the bed we sleep in smells like poop."

Gloria changed the subject. "How about Christmas presents around here. What do you want Santa to bring you?"

Zach shoved a whole cookie in his mouth. "There isn't a Santa."

Haley pounded her fist on the table and shook the plate of cookies. "Yes, there is! Zach says there isn't going to be Christmas this year."

"Of course there's going to be Christmas," Gloria said.

"Even for us?" Haley asked.

"Especially for you," Gloria said, squeezing her shoulders.

"Tell him," Haley said, looking at Zach.

"Christmas is alive and well," Gloria said.

"Fine," Zach said. "Whatever you say."

"A skeptic," Gloria said.

"Worse," Miriam said. "A Christmas skeptic."

"What's a skeptic?" Zach said.

"Someone who questions whether something is real or not," Gloria said. "A Christmas skeptic questions the realness of Santa and the spirit of Christmas."

Haley gaped at her. "What's gonna happen to him?"

"Well," Gloria said, "hopefully the spirit of Christmas will sweep through this place in such a powerful and mighty and magical way that Zach will believe again."

"Will it hurt?" Haley asked.

"Maybe," Miriam said. "But I doubt it."

I cashed out my tips at the end of the night and opened the back door. It was snowing again and I ran across the nearly empty lot. I unlocked my car and slid in, putting the key in the ignition. The car rumbled to and I looked behind me to back up, screaming as my eye caught a shape in my backseat. I threw the car in park and reached back for a tiny dress with wings that was propped up against the seat. What in the world? Who put this . . . ? How did they get into my car? It was locked! I reached for a sack next to it and found a command station building set. An envelope sat on top of it and I pulled it out, looking for a note. There were five twenty dollar bills inside and nothing else.

My heart thumped loudly in my ears. I looked over the parking lot but no one was around. I leaned over the seat and felt for any piece of paper that could have slid onto the floor. I got out of the car and looked around and beneath it. There wasn't anything. I sat in the car and held the dress in my lap. I could still hear my heart.

I turned off my headlights before I pulled into the driveway. The front door was locked and I was careful as I turned my key; I didn't want the kids to hear me and come running. I poked my head inside and saw Gloria smiling at me from the sofa. "Are the kids in bed?" I whispered. She nodded. I stepped through the door holding the bag and tiptoed around the sofa.

"What is going on?" Gloria asked.

I ran down the hall to make sure the kids were asleep and closed their doors behind me. "I can't believe it. You won't believe it," I said, throwing my coat on the couch. "Where's Miriam?"

"She left to walk the neighbor's dog. One of those hairless varieties named Sweetie, which she ain't by the way. If Miriam doesn't take her out by nine Sweetie pees all over the floor. Why are your eyes bugging out of your face?" I put the bag on the sofa and pulled out the dress with wings.

"Oh, she'll love it," Gloria said, whispering. "Where'd you get it?"

"In my backseat. Along with this building set and this," I said, handing her the envelope. Gloria opened it and looked at me, shocked. "I know! It's crazy."

"How'd they get in your car?"

"I have *no* idea," I said. "It's always locked."

"I've never heard of such a thing happening," she said. She hugged me and we bounced up and down together.

"Thank you, Gloria," I said. "Please thank Miriam, too." I turned and looked at the living room. "You cleaned." She smiled. I stepped around the corner to the kitchen. "You *really* cleaned."

"It's actually the only thing that Miriam can do," she said. She opened the closet for her coat. "You should know that your ex-husband showed up."

What a way to end the night. I felt my shoulders sink. "Claiming visitation?"

She nodded. "He was squawking but Miriam shut him up."

I leaned on the back of the couch. "I'm so sorry. He hasn't paid child support in months but loves to take me to court claiming abuse of power, overstepping my parental authority or whatever." Gloria put on

267

her coat and began buttoning it. "I don't know why I married him. I look back on it and still can't believe it."

She finished the last button and looked at me. "We can't live our lives looking back; if we did we'd turn into a pillar of salt." She pulled on her hat. "I've seen quite a few of his kind over the years. I've noticed that they just seem to fade away over time." I couldn't imagine Brad fading away. "Now we'll be back tomorrow, too, because I know you're working that insurance Christmas party."

"How'd you know that?"

"Zach told me," she said, smiling. "We'll be here at noon. You go on at twelve thirty, right?"

"Yes," I said, opening the door. She walked out and I pushed my head outside. "I forgot to ask. How were the kids?"

"They were great," she said. "You should be proud of those two." I closed the door and looked over my house. It hadn't been this clean in months. I sat on the sofa and held the dress and wings, building set, and money. I still couldn't believe it. The envelope I'd put under the tree caught my eye and I reached for it, pulling out the shredded pieces.

I walked to the kitchen and got a pen and

some tape to piece the torn paper back together. I smoothed out the wrinkles and spread the paper as flat as I could get it. *Thank you,* I wrote.

Gloria pulled into her driveway and walked across the lawn to Miriam's house. She knocked on the door and let herself in. "Hello!" she yelled over the television.

Miriam swept into the living room wearing a long flowing pink robe and gold-colored house slippers and carrying a bowl full of popcorn.

"What did you put in the car?" Gloria said.

Miriam threw a handful of popcorn in her mouth. "A dress and wings."

Gloria snapped off the TV. "So who left the building set and money?"

ELEVEN

Jason's phone rang before he was awake on Sunday morning. "Jason. It's Louis."

Why would his headhunter call on a Sunday? Jason strained to see his clock. "What's up?"

"Your interview needs to move."

Jason threw an arm over his eyes. "To when?"

"Tomorrow morning," Louis said.

Jason leaned up on one arm. "Why? What's wrong with Tuesday?"

"Sal Rubin needs to go out of town so all the interviews have shifted. They sent an e-mail Friday but my server was down. I just read it. He's leaving midmorning so they scheduled you at ten. If you get past Rubin you'll interview with Chip Holmes Tuesday at three."

"I have to be there for two days?"

"It would have been one but what can you

do? These things happen. Can you make it?"

"It takes seven hours to drive," Jason said. "I'd have to leave today."

"This job is yours to claim," Louis said. "Your profile is perfect. What do you want to do?"

Jason flopped his head back on the bed. "I'll be there," he said. He hung up and started to dial the number for Marshall to see if he could borrow his car earlier than expected but hung up and called information first. "Betty's Bakery," he said. The restaurant didn't open until noon on Sundays; Jason worried no one would be in yet. The operator connected him and a man answered. "Is Rosemary working?" he asked.

Craig was doing stock inventory and writing a list of supplies. "No. She's not in."

"Can I leave a message for her?"

"Yep."

"This is Jason. Can you tell her I can't make it tomorrow? I've been called for a job interview and have to leave right away but I'll be back Wednesday. Can we have coffee then?"

"Got it." Craig scribbled Rosemary's name on a take-out order sheet and wrote, *Jason can't make it tonight. Job interview. Back Wednesday.* He thumbtacked it to the message and scheduling board and didn't notice that it was Rosemary's day off. She'd never see it and no one else would pay attention to it.

"How can they pay that much money to a young kid?" Marshall asked, handing over his car keys.

"Big firm and lots of clients," Jason said. "I'd be stupid to blow off this interview."

"I agree."

"Sorry to leave you in a lurch the week of Christmas."

"Don't be. You've been waiting for this." He watched Jason reorganize his backpack. "You don't seem very excited."

Jason zipped the pack and slung it over his shoulder. "I think I am."

"You think?"

"All through college I thought I needed this, this, and this. Now I think I want something more." He opened Marshall's garage door. "That doesn't make any sense."

But it did. Marshall watched Jason back out of the garage and had the sense that in spite of himself he was finally hearing.

The party that evening was easy to work (they all ate the same thing and I never had to input one order) but it paid less than I could have made on a regular shift with tips. "It's honest money," my mom would say. "Take it and run."

Ann and Lori and I cleaned up and were out the door by nine. I was whipped. We hurried across the parking lot to our cars and as I unlocked the door to slide inside, the view of something in my backseat took my breath. I reached for the bags and pulled out a football and Sorry game out of one, and a princess game, Barbie doll, and an envelope with two hundred dollars cash in the other. I screamed and spun in my seat, looking at the cars and buildings around me. I put the key in the ignition and the car made a rer-rr-ing sound, the motor trying to turn over but not starting. "Oh, no! Not tonight," I said, trying the key again. The engine finally roared and I headed for home pounding the seat beside me. "I can't believe this!" I shouted. "I can't believe it!"

I turned off my headlights before pulling into the driveway again and threw the car in park. I was careful as I opened the front door. "Psst," I said, looking for Gloria and Miriam. Gloria stepped around the corner from the kitchen. "Are the kids in bed?" She nodded, waving me in. I ran inside carrying the bags and fell down on the floor.

"Is that more stuff?" Gloria whispered.

I nodded, sitting up. "Where's Miriam?"

"Naked dog."

I pulled the gifts from one bag and Gloria dug through the other one, pulling out the princess game, Barbie doll, and the envelope of cash.

"Gloria," I said, sitting up on my knees. "Do you believe in miracles?"

Gloria counted the money in the envelope. "You better believe I do."

Gloria didn't bother to knock on Miriam's door. She swung it open and marched to the living room, standing in front of the TV to block Miriam's view. "A football and Sorry game. That's what you left, right?"

"Yes," Miriam said, her eyes getting big with anticipation.

Gloria held up her fingers one at a time and counted off the list. "Then who left the princess game, Barbie, and wad of cash?!" Miriam smacked her head. "I have a plan," Gloria said. A miracle was afoot and she was determined to get to the bottom of it.

Dolly stepped inside my house Monday morning and noticed boxes lining the walls. "Just packing up books and stuff we don't use that often," I said.

She grunted and shook her head. "Any

closer to finding a place?"

I reached for my coat and put it on. "Not yet but I'm calling and looking every day."

Haley heard Dolly's voice and ran down the hall, throwing herself into her legs. "Dolly!" she said, taking hold of her hands. "Mom said you're watching us! We're going to have so much fun today."

"That's exactly what I said to myself this morning. I even wondered if you could come to my house and help me make and decorate Christmas cookies."

"Yes! Yes! Yes!" Haley said, wrapping her arms around her again.

Dolly laughed and patted her back. I finally found a neighbor as I was packing up to move. Sad, really.

When Jason got back into the car after his first interview he knew he had the job. It went so well that Sal Rubin would have adopted Jason if possible. He didn't want to head back to his friend's place but he didn't want to walk around the city, either, so he leaned his head back and closed his eyes. He had another full day to think about Rosemary and her smile and about a job that was going to give him everything he'd ever wanted.

■ ■ ■ ■

I made my rounds to the table of mechanics, Clayton, Julie and their kids, the insurance execs from the agency up the street, the old man with the ill-fitting teeth, the Asian college students, Lovey Love (who was an angel) and his mother, and finally Tamara. She was there earlier than usual. I wondered if she'd even show up since her new job had started. I set a day-old cinnamon pastry and a cup of coffee in front of her and knelt down next to her table, pulling something from my apron. "Merry Christmas," I said.

She stared down at the envelope and pulled it to her. "Christine, why did —"

"It's Christmas," I said, stopping her.

She opened the envelope and covered her mouth. "I can't," she said, moving the ticket toward me.

"Yes, you can," I said, sliding it back. "It's Christmas and they're your kids and you love them and would give anything to see them. It's a round-trip bus ticket but you'll have to book the return date yourself."

She started to cry and her voice came out in cracks and whispers. "But how did you —"

276

I stopped her. "My mom always said God makes a way. I never got that. I still don't totally get it but hope I'm getting closer." Tears streamed down her face and she held the napkin to her eyes. "Will you go?"

She leaned out of the booth to hug me. "Thank you," she said. She brought the napkin to her face and her hands trembled. "I'm so scared."

"They love you. They over-the-moon love you."

She smiled and picked up the ticket, looking at me through watery tears. It was the best money I'd ever spent.

I was going to take the kids to Glory's Place while I went out with TS but Dolly insisted they stay with her. "We had such a day," she said.

"We brought some cookies home," Zach said, holding up what looked like the results of a baking experiment gone wrong. I picked up a green and red sprinkled one that I was told was an elf on a pogo stick and ate it with gusto.

"Dolly said I could take some to Jason," Haley said.

"Who's Jason?" I asked.

"At Glory's Place. He's my half boyfriend. Remember?"

I hadn't but pretended I did. Dolly said she'd be back before six and I ran to the bathroom to shower and get ready. While in the shower I realized this wasn't the ideal way to tell TS I had children but then chastised myself for never bringing them up until now. When isn't it a good time to talk about my children?

My brown sweater was clean so I put it on and a pair of jeans. I wondered if that was the best outfit considering I wore jeans to work every day and held open my closet door looking for another option. "You're pretty, Mom," Haley said. She was dressed in her pink princess gown and brown rain boots. "He'll think you're pretty, too." That was good enough for me and I closed the closet door.

There was plenty of Gloria's day-old chicken and rice casserole for the kids. I warmed it up and sat with them at the table, watching the clock. Five thirty, five thirty-five, five forty. "Mom, can I have another cookie?"

Five fifty. He's wasn't going to be early. "Can I have some more milk?"

I checked my lipstick and hair. Five fifty-five. Dolly let herself in.

Six o'clock. "Can I have another cookie? Pleaaase?"

I stood at the door and looked out. Six ten, six fifteen. Six twenty.

"Maybe he worked late," Dolly said. "What time does he get off?"

"I don't know," I said, sitting on the sofa. "I don't know where he works."

Six thirty. "The roads are slippery," Dolly said. "On the news they said we're getting six inches tonight."

Six forty-five. Dolly sat at the table. "Can you call him?"

"I don't know his number," I said. "I don't even know his name yet." I looked at her. "How stupid is that?"

"Not stupid at all," she said, smiling. "I never knew my husband's name for four whole months." She watched me fidget on the sofa. "He'll probably call."

I laughed and covered my face with my arms. "He doesn't have my number! It gets better all the time, doesn't it?"

She got up and sat next to me. "You think a lot of this young man, don't you?"

I felt my throat tighten and nodded. "I don't know why. I don't even know him."

"But there's something about him that you feel you know."

I nodded. "I don't know what it is."

"It's just that thing people have when they're falling in love," she said.

I shook my head. "I'm not falling in love. I've been burned so many times that I *know* I am *not* falling in love. Plus, this hurts too much to be love. Just some wild thought I had."

She reached over and patted my hand. "Pain is part of love, Christine. I don't think we'd recognize love without it."

Before Jason's second interview, a woman who looked like she was in her forties showed him around the building, complete with cafeteria on the bottom floor. "There's a workout facility on the eighth floor," she said. "And a coffee bar on the tenth that overlooks the city." Her heels clicked on the shiny floors as she pointed out the board-room, meeting room, and break room. Jason couldn't tell if she liked her job; she was all business and brains and tight A-line skirt.

"Any questions?" she said, riding the elevator back to the twentieth floor.

"Do you like it here?"

"This building has everything we need right here," she said. "I forgot to show you the mail fulfillment and copying center."

"But do you like it?"

She watched the numbers light up above the elevator doors. "It pays great and I have two children. I love it here."

She walked him to Chip Holmes's office and that was the last Jason saw of her tight skirt. As suspected, the second interview was a formality only. After several minutes of answering inane questions, Chip extended his hand and offered Jason the job.

"Turn the car on, Gloria! I'm freezing!" Miriam sank lower in the passenger seat and pulled a blanket up to her chin.

Gloria unscrewed the cap on the thermos and poured black coffee into a cup. "We'll be conspicuous sitting here in a running car. Here. Drink that."

Miriam took the coffee and swallowed hard. "Why did I let you make the coffee? I can't believe you talked me into this. This is absurd. We've sat here for more than an hour and no one has even walked by Christine's car."

Gloria pulled her scarf up over her nose. "Don't you want to know who else is leaving gifts in her car?"

"Not if it means that I lose my extremities and will be up all night peeing. You don't own the market on being nice, you know."

Gloria saw a man walking toward them and shouted, "Here comes somebody!" They each dove to the center of the seat and clunked their heads together.

"Why didn't you go *that* way?" Miriam boomed, sitting up.

They gasped when they saw the man near Christine's car and dove toward the center a second time, nursing their heads again in the aftermath.

"He's getting in his *own* vehicle," Miriam said. "We are not built for a stakeout."

"No, we are not," Gloria said.

"For heaven's sake, Gloria! Start the car!"

"How many times do I have to say someone will notice?"

"At least let me have the snack bag again. Maybe I can store food away like a groundhog in hibernation and stay warm."

"Get down, get down!" Gloria whispered. She ducked in her seat and peered over the steering wheel. "That's our guy. I'm sure of it."

Miriam stretched her neck up to see a man pulling a bag from his trunk. They watched as he pulled out another bag and left them sitting by the rear passenger door of Christine's car before leaping into his running car and pulling away. Gloria and Miriam tumbled from the car and ran across the parking lot. "Why'd he leave them sitting here this time?" Gloria asked, wrapping her scarf tighter around her neck.

"Maybe he was on to us," Miriam said, pulling open one of the bags. She put her hand over her nose. "What is that smell?"

Gloria opened the second bag and flinched. She reached in and pulled out a package of ground beef. "Smells like it went bad weeks ago," she said, throwing it back into the bag.

"Rubbish!" Miriam said, gagging. "We've been waiting around for a litterer!"

Gloria picked up a bag and headed to the Dumpster at the far end of the parking lot. She looked at Miriam. "You bring that one."

Miriam covered her nose with her scarf. "I have a sensitive gag reflex."

Gloria glared at her and Miriam was certain smoke came out of her nostrils. "Pick up that bag."

Miriam picked the bag up and held it away from her. "You are a bully, Gloria Bailey."

The Dumpster lid clanged as Gloria lifted it open. She hurled her bag inside and then Miriam's. They ran to the side of the Dumpster when they heard voices coming out the back door of Betty's. Miriam covered her nose with her scarf and held her breath as Gloria watched Karen get into her car. Gloria pulled her cell phone out of her pocket and dialed a number. Miriam removed her scarf and exhaled as she talked. "Who are you calling?" She quickly inhaled, shoving the scarf over her nose again.

"We need to pick up Zach and Haley so we can see what's going on."

My cell phone rang as I was leaving. Gloria said she and Miriam would bring the kids home from Glory's Place. I grabbed my coat while we talked and waved at Spence as I headed for the back door. The restaurant phone rang and Spence yelled at me over the noise of the dishwasher and vacuum to answer it. I hung up with Gloria and picked up the restaurant phone, covering my other ear to hear the person on the line. "Betty's," I said, yelling over the noise of the kitchen.

The person said something but I couldn't hear. He was on a cell phone and between the bad connection and the noise of the kitchen I could only make out every other word. "What?"

"Rosemary there . . . ?"

"Rosemary's not in," I said, trying to move where I could hear.

"Can I . . . her number?"

"We can't give personal numbers out," I said.

"Can . . . I . . . note?"

"Sure." I grabbed a napkin and dug for a

pen in my purse.

"Had . . . interview. Got it. I . . . really . . . talk to her."

"Okay. And who is this?" I never made out the name. "She'll get it tomorrow," I said, yelling over the noise of the vacuum that Lori pushed back and forth next to me. I hung up the phone and stepped around the corner. Spence was mopping the floor in front of the message board. Rosemary wouldn't be in until tomorrow anyway. I shoved the napkin in my purse and headed to my car.

Gloria held Miriam close to the Dumpster so the employees leaving Betty's wouldn't see them. "Where is Christine?" Miriam asked, gasping for air. She took another deep breath and covered her mouth, gagging.

"You sound like a dog," Gloria said. She held her finger to her lips when she saw Christine walk to her car and climb inside. "She must be looking at our gifts," Gloria said.

Miriam uncovered her mouth and exhaled loudly as she whispered, "What's taking so long?" She inhaled and covered half her face.

Gloria turned to look at her. "You are the

most annoying person I've ever been on a stakeout with. Could you just breathe like a normal person?" The car moved across the parking lot and onto the road. Miriam exhaled like she'd just come up from the bottom of the sea. Gloria grabbed her wrist and pulled her toward the car.

I ran the bags to the back deck and shoved them inside the utility shed. My heart was still throbbing when Zach and Haley ran through the front door. "My half boyfriend wasn't there tonight," Haley said. "He had a job interview."

I wasn't listening. I told the kids to run get their pajamas on and when the lights flipped on in the bedrooms I grabbed Gloria's and Miriam's hands. "A model airplane was left in my car," I said, whispering. "Along with a game for Zach and a jewelry box and package of princess shoes for Haley." They smiled and squeezed my hands, nodding. "The second bag had two little stuffed dogs, a card game, two kids' movies, and an envelope with three hundred dollars cash." I pulled the envelope from my apron pocket and showed it to them. Their faces fell. Zach and Haley popped into the room and Gloria and Miriam moved for the door.

"How's that spirit of Christmas coming along?" Gloria asked, hugging Zach good-bye.

He shrugged. "Mom told me there won't be any gifts this year. How's yours?"

Gloria's eyes beamed. "Shooting out my fingertips!"

Miriam sat in the car and stared at the house. "We're not crazy, right?"

"It depends on who you're talking to," Gloria said. "But we never took our eyes off that car."

Miriam turned to look at her. "So how'd those gifts get in there?"

"When we took the garbage to the Dumpster."

"Are you suggesting that the refuse man was a distraction? On purpose?"

Gloria rested her forehead on the steering wheel. "That's the only time our backs were to that car."

"So we pick up the refuse and someone slips a bag in her car and vanishes into thin air?"

Gloria shrugged. "There are some things I don't think we're *supposed* to know."

For once in their lives they drove home in silence.

TWELVE

The bell above the florist shop door rang as Marshall pushed it open Wednesday morning. "Morning, Dwight!"

Dwight stepped from behind the counter and walked to a refrigerated display at the other side of the store. "Marshall, this is the most beautiful bouquet this store has ever sold."

He pulled the vase of flowers from the case and Marshall smiled. "Wow, those are beautiful."

"They come with a beautiful price, too," Dwight said. "I don't think you're ready for it."

Marshall took the bouquet from him. "It's okay, whatever it is. A man is married to a woman like Linda only once."

Dwight moved to the cash register. "That's what they tell me. Maybe wife number three will stick for me."

Marshall turned the bouquet to take a

good look. "Remind me again of what's in here."

Dwight pointed to each variety. "Lisianthus, peony, orchid, rose, lily of the valley, stephanotis, and of course hydrangea. Absolutely gorgeous." He rang up the flowers and watched Marshall's face. "You know, Marshall, people don't come in here and pay a hundred and forty dollars for a bouquet. The least you could do is react."

"They are stunning and beautiful and the perfect anniversary gift. I would have paid double that."

"Now you tell me," Dwight said, taking the money. "I need to wrap these."

"No, you don't."

"Are you taking them to the store? I'd like people to see these amazing flowers as they are. Have someone take pictures." He bundled them as if they were going on a ski trip and handed them to Marshall. He opened the door and a shot of cold air blew into the store. "Happy anniversary, Marshall."

My car's motor made a rer-rr-ing sound again that morning when I turned the key. I tried it again, hoping it would start as it had on previous days but after several attempts it wouldn't do anything. The kids and I ran to Dolly's door and rang the bell. She didn't answer. Haley rang it again and I peered through the door. All the lights were off. "Okay, back in the house," I said. Zach opened our door and I grabbed the phone to call Betty's. Craig answered. "My car won't start. I'll take the bus in."

"The bus!" Haley screamed. "Hurray." I wrapped a scarf around each of their necks and pulled their hats further down on their heads for the walk to the bus station.

It was a fifteen-minute walk and when we approached the bus stop my feet were freezing. We waited for the stoplight to change so we could cross the street and I kept my head down out of the wind. "Hey, it's Jason," Haley said. I saw the bus coming and grabbed Haley's hand so we could cross the road. "Zach, look!" She waved at a car beside us and I turned to look as it pulled away. "That was my half boyfriend, Mom. He must be back."

"Maybe he's headed to Glory's Place," I said, leading them across the street to the bus stop. We jumped on the bus and Haley led us to seats across from an older man holding flowers. I tried to move my feet inside my tennis shoes. They were so cold. I rested the back of my head against the window. What was wrong with my car? How could I pay for it, Haley's hospital bill, and a deposit on a place to live? The thought overwhelmed me and I closed my eyes.

"Those are pretty," Haley said.

"Thank you," the man said.

"My mom loves those kind of flowers." I opened my eyes to see her point to a hydrangea.

"Those are my wife's favorite, too," the man said.

"Are those for her?" Haley asked.

"Yes. It's our anniversary today."

"Congratulations," I said. "How many years?"

"This is number forty-four."

"Wow! That's older than my mom," Haley said.

He laughed and I squeezed Haley's leg, giving her a look to stop bothering him. "Do you have kids?" she asked, ignoring my signal.

"Three. And I always thought my wife was beautiful but she was really, really, really beautiful when she had them."

"Why?" Haley asked.

He shrugged. "Because there's just something about a mother and her children." He looked at me and smiled.

"What does she look like?"

He leaned toward her. "No offense to your

mom but my wife is the most beautiful woman I've ever seen. Her eyes are as blue as the sky and when she was young her hair was as dark as night. It turned gray, of course, but then that ushered in a whole new era of beautiful. She never liked it. She didn't care for the wrinkles either but I think they only added to her beauty."

I looked at him and couldn't imagine a love that was long lasting or a man who would still be enamored with me after so many years together. What he was describing was how love was supposed to be. My eyes filled with tears and I turned my face before they fell. The bus stopped and the man stood. "It was nice meeting you," he said.

"Nice to meet you," Haley said. He bent over and whispered something in her ear. She took the flowers and he walked off the bus.

"Wait!" I said, trying to stand. The driver pulled away and I turned to look at Haley.

"He said his wife would want you to have these," she said, holding the flowers out to me.

I turned to see out the window and tears streamed down my face as I watched the man walk into the cemetery.

■ ■ ■ ■

Jason closed the car door and walked across the grounds to Marshall. He had been a sophomore in college when his grandmother died. Was that only five years ago? "I drove to the store. I didn't think you'd come here so early."

"That's okay. What time did you get back?"

"Midnight."

"Did you get the job?"

Jason nodded. "Where're the flowers? I thought you ordered some weeks ago."

"I gave them to a young mother on the bus."

"You gave them away?" Marshall nodded and Jason laughed. "They would have been too fancy for Grandma anyway so she would have liked that."

Marshall smiled looking at the tombstone. "That's what I said."

I was an hour late to work. I rushed through the back door to the front counter and set the flowers down. "My car won't start. I'm sorry," I said, to anyone who was listening.

Karen picked up the coffeepot and noticed the flowers. "Gorgeous," she said. "Where'd you get them?"

I headed to the kitchen. "A man gave them to me on the bus."

"Which bus and what kind of man?!"

I laughed and hung up my coat, grabbing an apron off the hook. Gloria and Miriam were eating at one of my tables. "What happened?" Gloria said, wiping her mouth.

"Car wouldn't start," I said, filling her coffee.

She dove for her purse. "Did you tow it?" I shook my head. "I know just the guy. He's been working on my cars for years. Do you have AAA?" I shook my head again. "No bother. He'll go to your place." She started to dial the number. "His name is Jack Andrews."

"One of the mechanics who come in here?" She nodded. "I don't think I can afford to get it fixed right now," I said, whispering to her. "I need an apartment. . . ." She waved me out of her face and started talking to someone.

"He won't charge you," Miriam said.

"How can he not charge me?"

"It's his thing," she said. "Just like this" — she waved her hands in front of Gloria — "is her thing." I opened my mouth and Miriam stopped me. "Gloria has discovered over the years that most people aren't looking for a handout. They're just looking for a hand. So shut up and take the hand." I tried to say something but she pointed behind me to a table.

Clayton, Julie, and their kids sat in a booth and I grabbed a pot of coffee and two cups. Julie looked radiant in a green sweater and with a bright red scarf around her head. "Well, who picked out that beautiful scarf today?" I asked.

"I did," Ava said. "I thought she'd look like Mrs. Santa in it but she still looks like Mom."

Julie laughed and I set the cups on the table, filling them with coffee. "How are you?" I asked.

"I think I look better than I feel," she said, whispering to me. "But that's okay." She spoke louder so her kids could hear. "Christmas is two days away and I can hardly wait." She smiled at Clayton and I knew she didn't just say that for the kids' sakes. I had a feeling that from now on every Christmas, birthday, sunrise, and rainy day would be a thing of beauty for her.

Jason swung open the door and scanned the restaurant. I watched him walk to the counter and lean into the vase of flowers to see if they were real. He beamed when he saw me at the waitress station. "Hey! I'm so sorry I had to bolt town like that." My face was blank. "They moved my interview." What was he talking about? "Did you get my messages?" I shook my head and he threw his arms in the air. "I knew they were just going into a black hole. I called Sunday before you were open and left a message and then I called yesterday."

I put my tray on my hip. He left town! "You had a job interview?"

He looked at his watch. "I have to get back to work but yes!"

"Did you get it?"

"Yeah."

I forced a smile. "Congratulations. When do you start?" I wanted to say, "Why don't you find a job here?" Or, "Please don't go" but I didn't.

He looked at me and smiled. "Will we ever get to have coffee?"

Wilson's was packed that day. Jason helped Matt in menswear for the better part of the morning and couldn't keep up with the mess in the fitting rooms. He hauled a wad of pants and shirts out of an empty room and dumped them onto a counter to hang.

"Hey, where you been?"

He turned to see Marcus standing behind

him. "Hey, dude. How's your shot coming along?"

"Nothing but net," Marcus said. "And Dalton can't throw and none of the girls know how to do it, either. Where you been?"

Jason slung a pair of pants over a hanger and hung it on the rack. "I had to go for a job interview."

"Where at?"

"At a big firm that does accounting for lots of businesses."

Marcus slapped his head. "I don't even know what you're talking about! Will you still work at Glory's Place and play basketball?"

Jason hung another pair of pants. "No. It's pretty far from here."

Marcus was quiet and looked around the department for his mom. "See you later."

Matt stepped beside Jason holding three ties. "Hey, a special shipment of these ties was due today. Could you see if they're here? These are the last of them we have."

Jason ran down the stairs and into the shipping department. It was empty. He went through the swinging doors to the mailroom and stopped. "Hold it. Your name is . . . Tina?" She shook her head. "Tonya?" She raised her eyebrows. "Tammy?"

"Close enough. Tamara."

He snapped his fingers. "Now I remember! I'm looking for a box of ties." She pointed to a box on the opposite counter. "How's it going down here?"

"I like it," she said, sorting through a stack of mail in her hands. "You've been gone."

"I had a job interview."

She slid envelopes into slots on the wall. "Did you get it?" He nodded. "And you're bursting with excitement!" He laughed and leaned onto the counter. "Are you glad you got it?"

"I thought I would be but I'm all messed up. Ever been like that?"

"You don't even want to go there with me!" She slid more mail into the slots and looked over her shoulder at him. "What's the problem?"

He watched her work and wondered why he would tell her anything but couldn't think of any reason not to tell her everything. He had the sense that she knew far more than he did. "A girl. A woman."

"Here or there?"

"She's here. The job's there."

"What does she say?"

He laughed and jumped onto the counter, sitting on top of it. "We've never even been out together." She stopped working and looked at him. "So what's the problem, right?"

"No, that's a pretty big problem," she said. "If you go you'll never know, will you?" He nodded. "But if you stay and the whole thing's a bust then you'll kick yourself for what you gave up."

"Right."

She picked up another stack of mail and began sorting it. "Jobs are always there and there and over there but the possibility of love is *not* always there."

"She might not even like me."

Tamara smiled. "I bet she will."

He picked up the box and swung open the door. "If I don't see you tomorrow. Hope you have a great Christmas. Are you here or . . ."

"I'm going home," she said.

The lunch crowd fell off a little after one and I remembered the note I'd taken for Rosemary. I went to my locker and pulled the napkin out of my purse. The bulletin board was empty except for the schedule and a solitary note in the middle of the board. I glanced at it as I thumbtacked the napkin up: *Rosemary, Jason called. Job interview. Can't do coffee. Back Wednesday.* I looked at the note I had scribbled on the napkin, also to Rosemary, and laughed out loud.

"Christine!" Karen was behind me. "There's a woman out here asking for you."

I yanked the note down off the board and shoved it and the napkin into my apron pocket as I stepped around the corner. Mom was in front of the counter checking out the pastries and wearing a navy blue coat and a green scarf. Her red hair had recently been cut and was cropped short around her face. "Hey!" I said, running to her. "What are you doing? You were coming in tomorrow. I have to work and I'm not ready!"

She wrapped her arms around me and held on tight. "That's why I came early. Now I can make candy and cookies with the kids and help you get ready for Christmas." She held me at arm's length. "You look so pretty!"

"An apron always brings out my eyes."

She slapped my arm and looked into the display case. "This place is great! Cream cheese bear claws? I haven't seen one of those in ages!"

"Sit down and I'll get you one," I said.

"I don't need a cream cheese bear claw. I just had lunch an hour ago and I want to see my grandchildren."

"Mom, you haven't gained an ounce in twenty years. Eat the bear claw and then see your grandchildren." I popped a bear claw into the microwave for a few seconds before setting it and a cup of coffee in front of her.

She took a bite and shook her head. "This is unbelievable. I've never had one this good. Is it made here?"

"All the baked goods are made here. Betty's son came up with that recipe," I said. She took another bite and I leaned onto the table. "Mom, you are never going to believe what's been happening the last few days."

"Well, this must be Mom, right?" Betty walked toward me and I nodded.

Mom smiled and turned her head to greet Betty and her eyes bulged. "Elizabeth?"

"Jeanette!" Mom stood and Betty gave her a hug. "Let me wrap my mind around this," Betty said, looking at her. "You're Christine's mother?"

I sat in the seat and watched them. "You know each other?"

"I worked in Elizabeth's bakery. She taught me everything I know."

Betty sat down and stared at her. "Jeanette, I swear you're as pretty today as you were at seventeen when you and Dennis were chasing each other around the kitchen." Mom tried to smile but her face was stricken. "I would have given anything to keep your mother but she and Dennis broke up and I lost my best little baker." She threw her hands in the air. "What a world! Fast-forward more than twenty-five years later and I'm working with your daughter." She grabbed my face in her hands. "And she is as delightful as you were. You can be proud of this one."

"I am," Mom said.

I was still so confused. "Did you work in *this* town?" I asked. There was so much about my mother's youth that she never talked about.

"Right up the road," Betty said. "At my first bakery. You and your folks only lived here a couple of years, right?"

"That's right," Mom said. "Then we moved north."

"I was so sad to see you go and Dennis was beside himself. He tried to act cool but I knew. He was such a mess at that time. You remember. And it only got worse for a few years."

Mom poked at the bear claw on her plate. "Where is he now?"

"He had a massive heart attack and died eight years ago."

Mom was quiet for a while, looking at her. Then she said, "I'm sorry, Elizabeth."

"You need to call me Betty. Nobody calls me Elizabeth anymore. Betty was much less to pay for on a sign." She grabbed Mom's hand. "My mind is racing! Did you get married?"

"Yes. My husband will be here tomorrow afternoon."

"Then you need to bring your dad by as well, Christine," she said, looking at me.

"Richard's not my dad. Mom married him seven years ago."

"Well, still bring him by," she said, throwing her hands in the air again. Craig called to her from behind the counter. He was waving papers in the air. She stood and leaned over to hug Mom. "We *have* to catch up and I *must* tell you wonderful things about your daughter. Duty calls for now."

"Bye, Betty," Mom said, watching her walk away. "She hasn't changed."

"And that's a good thing, right?"

She nodded. "It's great. She's always been one of my favorite people."

"Mine, too," I said.

She took another bite of bear claw and pushed the plate away. "Okay, let's keep this excitement rolling along. Where are my grandchildren?"

■ ■ ■ ■

Jason carried the gift boxes that hadn't been picked up and loaded them into the back of Marshall's car. "Are you sure this isn't too many?" Dalton asked. "No, it's fine," Jason said. He ran inside the door for the last of the boxes.

"What are you doing?" Zach asked.

"Delivering these boxes for Miss Glory."

"Can I help you deliver them?"

"You're not allowed to leave the premises. Besides, you'd have a lot more fun here."

"You're back!" Haley slammed into his legs and hugged them tight. "I saw you this morning when we were walking to the bus stop and I said, 'He's back. He's back!' "

"Mom's car died," Zach said.

"But it was great because we got to ride the bus and an old guy gave Mom flowers," Haley said.

Jason stopped working and looked at her. "An old guy gave her flowers?"

Haley made a circle with her arms. "A huge bouquet of the world's most beautiful flowers."

He laughed and gave her a hug. "That is so cool."

"She was late going to work but I told her

that she was *supposed* to be late today so she could get the flowers."

"That's right," Jason said, giving her a high five.

The door opened and a blast of wintry air filled the vestibule. "Nana!" Haley shouted. Jason watched Zach and Haley fling themselves into a woman's body and she wrapped them in her arms.

"Hey! What'd Dalton say about not talking to strangers?" Jason said, teasing them.

"This is not a stranger," Haley said. "This is Nana."

"I assumed that," he said, sticking out his hand. "I'm Jason. Nice to meet you."

"I'm Jeanette," she said. "My daughter said she'd call so I could take the kids home."

"Dalton or Heddy probably talked with her," he said. He waved at Dalton and Jason turned to go, looking at Jeanette. She smiled and he walked out the door.

Judy pushed open the office door and smiled when she saw Marshall trying to find something on her computer. "Give up yet?"

"What's wrong with ledgers and paper files?"

"Nothing if you're a Pilgrim," she said.

He pulled off his glasses. "Is your vacation

about over?"

"You're the one who told me to stay home," she said, sitting on the chair in front of her desk. "So . . . happy anniversary. Did you take the flowers out yet?"

"I was en route with the flowers when I gave them to someone else."

"To who?" she asked, leaning forward.

"Get that grin off your face. To a young mother on the bus."

She shook her head and smacked it, trying to compute what he was saying. "What were you doing on the bus?"

"Jason had the car."

"Did he get the job?" Marshall nodded. "I suppose I shouldn't even ask if you've sat down for your talk yet?"

Marshall sighed. "Judy, I'm too old for change."

She slapped the desk. "Nobody's *ever* too old for change if the change is good. Don't blow this, Marsh."

"You sound like Linda. *Both* of my Lindas."

"That's because the three of us were always smarter than you."

"I know."

Gloria called a few minutes before I got off work and told me my car was in the back parking lot. "You mean it's fixed?" I asked, peeking out the door.

"Just a spark plug," Gloria said. "I didn't want you to ride the bus home so Miriam and I dropped it off."

"What do I owe Jack for his work?"

"Not a thing," she said.

I opened my mouth to say something but decided, like Miriam said, to take hold of the hand and shut up.

When we closed, Spence wrapped the vase of flowers in newspaper for me and held open the back door. I walked to the car and wondered how I'd get the flowers home without their toppling over. I put the key in the door and opened it, smiling as I sat down. Two envelopes sat on the backseat. I propped the flowers up against the front seat and reached for the envelopes. Five hundred dollars in cash was in the first envelope and the second had a one-hundred-dollar gift certificate to Wilson's, a one-hundred-dollar certificate to the grocery store, and a one-hundred-dollar gift card to the gas station. I could feel my hands trembling. I had enough money to pay Ed for all my back rent. My mind raced with the thought. Maybe we could stay in the duplex.

The scent of fresh-baked cookies filled the

living room as I opened the front door. Haley's and Zach's pajamas were covered with flour and I didn't even dare ask how many cookies they'd eaten. A plate full of Santa cookies sat on the counter along with my favorites, pecan balls. I set the flowers down on the table and unwrapped them before popping a pecan ball into my mouth, moaning as I chewed. "It's Christmas!" I said.

"Look," Haley said, holding up a pan. "Peanut butter fudge! Nana says it's your favorite."

"Did Nana also tell you it's her favorite, too?"

"Please tell me that you ate something else besides cookies and candy for dinner," I said, popping another pecan ball into my mouth.

"Shh," Mom said, looking at Zach and Haley. "Our secret."

"Fine," I said. "It's time to brush your teeth and read stories."

"But we still haven't watched *Rudolph* this year," Haley said.

I looked at my watch. It was nine o'clock but there was no way they were going to fall asleep knowing Nana, cookies, and candy were in the house. "All right. Brush your teeth and then run back out here for *Ru-*

dolph." They ran screaming through the hallway. I held up the pan of fudge. "You know this isn't nearly enough peanut butter fudge, right?"

I tucked Haley and Zach in his bed together a few minutes after Rudolph led Santa's sleigh through the night skies. It was just before ten. "Two more sleeps until Christmas," Haley said. "Will it matter to Santa if I'm sleeping in Zach's bed?"

Zach rolled his eyes. "There isn't a Santa. We don't even have a fireplace."

"No," I said, giving him a look. "It doesn't matter to Santa where you sleep. He'll know you're in here and will leave gifts for you." I kissed her face and snuggled Brown Dog under her chin.

"No, he won't," Zach said. I kissed his cheek and smiled.

I grabbed a blanket and pillow out of the hall closet and put them on the couch. I'd sleep there so Mom and Richard could take my room. Mom was sitting at the kitchen table, drinking a cup of tea with a pecan ball.

I sat down across from her and picked up another cookie. "When were you going to tell me, Mom?" She looked up at me. "When were you going to tell me that Dennis was my father?"

THIRTEEN

A tear fell down her cheek and she brushed it away. "When did you know?"

"When you saw Betty's face I knew something was wrong. Then at the mention of his name you looked like you were going to pass out."

"I never dreamed anything like this would ever —" She pressed a napkin into her eyes. "I was so afraid when you moved here with Brad that you would run into Dennis and somehow . . . I don't know."

So that's why she acted so angry when I moved here. "Does Betty know?" She shook her head. "Did he even know?"

Tears fell down her face and she used the napkin to wipe them away. "No. He was so into drugs at that time that . . ." She trailed off. "Your grandparents absolutely hated him. They had caught us smoking marijuana together and I thought your grandfather would go to jail the way he threw Dennis off our property. When they found out I was pregnant they went ballistic. They didn't need to because I knew. I wasn't ready to be a mother but Dennis *sure* wasn't ready for any sort of responsibility. He was sex and that's all." She was quiet and I knew it was more than she wanted to say. "Mom and I moved north and as soon as Dad found a job there he joined us. No one here ever knew."

"Did you ever want to tell him?"

She shook her head. "Not the way he was. He wouldn't have helped. He couldn't help. He didn't even have a job at the time. And I didn't want to see him because I was afraid we'd just fall back into . . . well . . ."

I couldn't imagine the girl my mother was talking about. "Does Haley look like him?"

She nodded. "Her eyes and nose, especially."

"Was he handsome?"

"Too handsome for his own good," she said. "Girls loved him and when the drugs took hold, watch out. He was invincible. He had too many girls."

"But you were his favorite," I said, watching her. "Maybe he would have changed for you."

She shook her head. "He wasn't ready."

"Do you hate him?"

"No," she said, swishing the napkin on the table in front of her. "I did for a long time. I wanted him to take as much responsibility as I did. I wanted him to grow up and do the right thing. For the longest time I thought he was the one who had it made. He could do whatever he wanted without any strings attached. He could go wherever he wanted without any obligation to anybody. But then you started to grow and I started hating him less because he wasn't the one who had it made. I was. I had this beautiful little obligation that hung on my leg and lit up when I entered the room." My eyes filled with tears at the sound of her voice. She wiped her face and twisted the napkin in her hands. "Before you came along I never felt a bursting sense of happiness when someone smiled at me or reached out for me. I never just sat and held a little life in my arms just because I loved the way it made me feel. I never knew what it was like to have my heart beat outside my body or feel it break with joy when someone came running to me to kiss a boo-boo. I never sat beside a crib and watched a tiny body breathe because that's what I wanted to do more than anything else at that moment." She looked up at me with wet, swollen eyes. "How could I hate him for that?" Her voice broke and I wiped a tear from my cheek. "I am so sorry, Christine. I know you wanted to know who your father was but I never thought of him as a father but only a sperm donor. I was so afraid that he'd reject you because he never knew about you. I couldn't bear that thought. I'm so sorry. Now it's too late and . . ."

I moved to the chair next to her and took her hand. "It's not too late, Mom. I have a grandmother I never knew about who, as it turns out, is one of my favorite people on the planet." She laughed and fell into me. For years I had wanted to know about this secret in the dark. I wanted to know what my father looked like, what he did for a living, which authors he read, what movies he watched, where he went for fun, and if he ever thought of me while doing any of those things. In all that time I never thought of my mother who held my hand while she moved through her life created by one heat-of-the-moment decision with stunning grace and courage. I assumed she held things from me like a child playing keep-away but never realized she was doing it for me, not against me. For far too long I didn't realize that she was indeed holding secrets, the greatest and most beautiful secrets of sacrifice, love, and life in her hand. We cried together and talked until the early morning hours.

Jason scrambled to keep up on the last day of shopping at Wilson's. He saw Marshall only in passing but promised to drop by the house after he delivered the last of the packages for Glory's Place.

He jumped in Marshall's car at six and held a local map on top of the steering wheel to find his way around. "Don't you have a GPS?" he had asked Marshall.

"Is that some kind of four-wheeler?" Marshall had responded.

Jason chuckled again at the response and slowed down at a street sign. The first house was well lit and ready for Christmas with a small tree in the front window. He rang the bell and left the box of goods with a grateful mother of three. The next house was only four blocks away and after several knocks he left the box between the storm and front door. An apartment complex housed two families who would receive boxes. Four children scurried around his legs like squirrels in the first apartment that smelled like tortillas and frijoles. They clamored for the box and Jason laughed as they squealed at the sight of new toothbrushes and socks! Two floors down Jason knocked on a door and a small face peeked through the crack of the open door. "Hey!" The door flew open. "It's you."

Jason smiled at Marcus. "And it's you! It's me and it's you!"

"What are you doing here? Christmas is coming, you know?"

Jason smiled at the mother and knelt down in front of Marcus. "I know. That's why I'm hurrying to deliver these gifts so I can get home and get to sleep!"

Marcus took the box and looked at his mother. "Can I?" She nodded and he lifted the lid. He pulled out a child's toothbrush and tube of toothpaste and small car and put them on the floor beside him. The rest of the contents were entirely too utilitarian and he handed the box to his mother. "You can have the rest," he said.

She laughed and held the box to her. "Thank you. He loves Glory's Place."

"He doesn't work there anymore," Marcus said. "He got a job far away so he can't play basketball anymore." The mother smiled and winked at Jason.

"I'll tell you what," Jason said. "If you practice your shots, I promise I'll come back and play with you from time to time."

"I'll take you down," Marcus said.

Jason opened the door. "That's big talk

from a kid who chucks nothing but air balls."

The last house on Jason's list was a few blocks from Wilson's. He pulled into the driveway and wrapped his coat around him. The temperature was dropping and snow was on the way. He knocked and the door flew open. "Jason!" Haley wrapped her arms around his waist and he laughed as she pulled him inside.

He smiled at the grandmother he'd met this morning and handed the box to her. "From Glory's Place. For the kids and their mom."

She put it under the tree and Jason looked at Haley. "So, any more strangers give you flowers or jewelry or a new princess palace?"

"No, you silly! People don't give princess palaces away. But come look at the flowers." She held his hand and led him to the table. "Ta-da!"

"Those are awesome," he said. He turned to go and noticed a picture on the sofa table. It was Zach and Haley with a woman. He leaned down to look at it and grabbed the photo in his hands. "Is *this* your mother!" Haley nodded and he looked up at the ceiling. "I am so stupid." Jeanette walked to his side and looked at him staring at the picture. "He gave the flowers to *her!*"

He shook his head, looking at the photo, and then smiled at Jeanette. "I didn't know Rosemary was their mother."

"Christine," Jeanette said. "That's Christine."

He stared at the photo and laughed. "Christine!" He bent over, laughing.

"What's so funny?" Haley asked, confused.

"I'm just so stupid," he said, hugging her.

"Mom says we shouldn't say that word."

"She's right!" He set the picture back on the table and smiled at Jeanette. "Christine looks just like you."

"That's quite a compliment," Jeanette said. "Because I've always thought she's beautiful."

"She is," he said.

He laughed out loud when he got into the car and dialed Marshall's number. The phone clicked over to voice mail. "I just found the perfect gift for Judy," he said, and hung up.

Marshall knocked on the door around eight. He felt ridiculous. Who visits someone unannounced on Christmas Eve? The lights around the door and railing lit up the porch and he could smell the scent of roast beef wafting under the door. The lock clicked and Marshall smiled at Matt. "Marshall! What in the world are you doing here?"

Marshall held a package in his hand. "I had this and thought maybe I should bring it by."

"Come on in," Matt said, moving out of the way. He called over his shoulder. "Hey, Mom, Marshall's here."

"Who?" a voice said behind Matt. Marshall knocked the snow off his boots on the porch mat and his heart pounded at the prospect of walking inside. "Marshall! Hello!" Gloria was wearing a red cardigan sweater covered with holly leaves and a white turtleneck.

"I'm sorry to stop by so late," Marshall said.

"Come on in," she said. "Would you like some eggnog or coffee?"

"No, nothing," he said, fumbling with the package in his hands. It fell and he bent over to pick it up.

"Well, sit down," she said, pointing to the sofa.

Miriam stuck her head out the kitchen door. "Marshall! You're just in time to eat."

"No, no," he said. *Good grief, who else is here?* he thought.

Matt's wife, Erin, carried a basketful of fresh rolls and set them on the kitchen table.

"Hi, Marshall," she said. "What are you doing out and about tonight?"

Gloria looked at him and he held out the package. "I saw this and . . . well, I thought you might like it."

She took it from him and laughed. "Well, what a surprise! I would never refuse a gift. How thoughtful." She tore into the paper and pulled out a hand-painted serving bowl. "This is lovely," she said, smiling.

Marshall stood in a rush. "It was at the store and . . . Judy saw it actually and thought you'd . . . well, I'll scoot out of here and let you eat." He opened the door.

"Marshall, why don't you stay and eat with us?" she asked, standing in the open doorway. "We're all family here."

"No, no. I should have called. I hope you have a merry Christmas."

She stepped onto the porch and wrapped her sweater tight around her. "Is everything okay, Marshall?"

He stopped on the stairs and turned to look at her. He hung his head and sighed. "I feel like a fool." She watched him stamp his foot up and down. "I don't know what I'm doing." She waited for more. "I'm too old to start dating again. The very notion makes me break out in a sweat." Gloria touched her hair, aware for the first time of what was happening. "I sent those ridiculous notes to you and I'm sorry." It felt like her legs were gone and she wondered if she had passed out and fallen inside the door. If she was speaking she couldn't hear a word she was saying. "I didn't have the character to show up at the gardens and I cursed myself for days. Then Judy and my daughter, Linda, found out about it and they cursed me, too. Linda's been after me since her mother died — especially the last two years — to get off my rump and well . . ." Gloria smiled and realized she no longer felt the wind or the cold.

"Marshall —" She stopped and he couldn't imagine what she would say. Whatever it was, he knew he deserved it. "It is an honor to be thought of so highly by someone I've respected for so long." He felt the weight tumble off his back and smiled. "Now, would you please come in out of the cold and eat with us?" He didn't move. "Unless you have somewhere else to go?"

"I don't," he said.

Betty was with her daughter and grandchildren so I never saw her on Christmas Eve. The restaurant closed early and as I cleaned the hallway outside Betty's office, I stepped inside, turning on the light. Dennis's face smiled out at me in several photos on her desk. Haley did have his eyes and nose and Zach seemed to have his square chin. I glanced from one photo to the next. He was handsome in all of them. I hugged Spence and Lori and the rest of the crew and bolted out the door for home.

Richard had arrived earlier in the day and had spent the afternoon playing games with Zach and Haley. He had willingly stepped into the role of grandfather and did it with ease. He doted after them as if they were part of his bloodline and I knew I should have been more grateful than I was for him. The kids ran to bed without a word of argument at nine o'clock sharp and I caught up with Richard as they fell asleep. When their mouths fell open and their hands hung limp over the side of the bed we went to the storage shed on the deck and hauled in the presents. It took me far too long to tell Richard the story of the gifts but I couldn't leave out a single word. Mom added her and Richard's gifts for the kids and the tree glowed brighter than ever with the bounty under its branches. A small noise stopped our work; we were afraid Zach and Haley was tiptoeing about. I ran to the door when we realized someone was knocking. I looked through the window and opened the door. "Ed?"

"I'm sorry it's so late, Christine."

"I actually thought of you last night and wanted to talk to you. Come on in." He stepped inside and nodded to Mom and Richard. "I wanted to talk about the back rent."

"That's why I'm here," he said. I had the feeling he was going to ask me to leave earlier than the end of next month. "Christine, if there's any way you could pay half of the back rent I'd be willing to let you stay."

Half! I had enough money to pay all of it. "But Ed, I owe you —"

He shook his head. "Half is fine." He put his hand on the knob and turned it.

"Thank you, Ed." He nodded and opened the door but I had to know more. "What changed your mind?"

He sighed. "My mother. She's very stubborn and persistent and set in her ways but she's also a good judge of people."

I wondered if I knew her from the restaurant. "Who's your mother?"

"The Bat Lady," he said, smiling, and closed the door.

Mom and Richard and I stayed up far too late and the kids woke up way too early.

"He came!" Haley squealed two feet from me. I jolted awake on the couch and saw her jumping up and down. She ran screaming down the hall. "He came! He came! Presents are everywhere!"

Zach raced to the living room and his mouth dropped open at the sight. "You said there wouldn't be any gifts."

I sat up and smiled. "They're not from me."

Mom entered, wrapping the belt around her robe, and Richard pulled a sweatshirt over his head. "I told you he would come," Haley said, jumping. "Gloria said the spirit of Christmas would sweep through here and it did and it made Zach believe! Just like she said!"

"I didn't even hear the old man," Richard said.

"I thought I heard something around two," Mom said. "But I fell right back to sleep."

"I heard him," Zach said.

"You did?" I asked, swinging my legs to the floor.

"Yes! I heard him and I snuck out of bed and saw him standing right here."

"You *saw* him?" Haley asked, amazed.

"I saw a piece of red," he said. "But he didn't stand there long. He was so fast that he disappeared real quick." He picked up a present. "This one's mine! Can we start, Mom?" I nodded and he handed a present to Haley.

"Open it," I said.

Mom turned on the video camera and Richard took still pictures as the kids ripped open their gifts. Haley shrieked when she lifted the princess dress from the box and Zach struck a quarterback's stance when he palmed the football. In minutes the living room was a colorful, glorious mess. Zach handed a present to me and I looked at Mom. "We weren't supposed to exchange."

"I don't need anything," she said, grinning.

I opened a box with a new pair of gloves, socks, and a beautiful blue sweater, another package contained two new books to read, and a third box held a new skillet and hand mixer. "So you don't have to hold the cord up," Mom said, referring to my mixer with the short in it.

Zach handed me a flat, flimsy gift, and I was careful as I opened it. He had wrapped a picture he had drawn on construction paper. We were in the snow building a snowman. I was the biggest, Zach the next biggest, and Haley was wearing a dress with wings. "You know just what I like," I said, hugging him.

Haley thrust a gift in my hand. "Wait until you see mine."

I opened the package and pulled out a hand-painted heart box like the one I'd seen at Wilson's. "Haley! This is so beautiful. Where did you get it?"

"My half boyfriend did it with me."

I looked over the box and lifted the lid. Even the inside was painted. "A kite, butterfly, flowers. All of my favorite things are here. If I could fit you and Zach inside here it'd be perfect!" She laughed and I hugged her tight.

Zach handed me a small gift and I looked at Mom. "No more gifts, Mom! What is this?"

"I have no idea," she said.

"Right," I said. I ran my finger along the tape and lifted the lid on a small velvet box. "Mom!" I lifted a diamond necklace from the box and held it in front of me. "This is gorgeous!"

"Who's it from?" she asked.

"You can stop playing now. I love it. Thank you."

"It's not from me," she said. I could tell by her face that she was oblivious. She looked at Richard.

"Don't look at me," he said.

I noticed a small tab of paper sticking up inside the box and lifted the velvet padding. Underneath was a tightly folded note. Haley jumped up next to me to take a closer look. *Merry Christmas,* I read. *Please bring Zach and Haley to Ashton Gardens today at noon.*

"Who left this?" I asked, looking at Mom and Richard.

"I have no idea," Mom said.

"I just got here yesterday," Richard said.

I looked at Zach and Haley.

"No clue, Mom," Zach said.

I laughed and touched the diamond. "So what we're saying is someone broke into my house and left this?"

"I wish we had break-ins like that," Richard said.

"Well, I'm not going to go. We were supposed to eat at noon."

"Christine!" Mom said. "We have all day to eat. Go to the gardens."

"But someone broke into my house. This is creepy and weird and a little unsettling."

She sat down next to me. "Richard and I will go with you." I started to protest and she squeezed my leg. "Christine, it's Christmas . . . and a diamond! I don't think it's creepy and weird but more like magical and mysterious."

■ ■ ■ ■

I was nervous when Richard drove into Ashton Gardens. "No one's here," I said. "Let's go back home."

"We're not even halfway in," Mom said.

Richard drove back toward the greenhouse and I saw a car parked outside. "Recognize that?" Richard asked. I shook my head. I'd never seen it before.

He parked beside it and Mom turned around to look at me. "Well, here we are!" She made it sound like we'd just arrived at an amusement park. "Are you ready?"

"No," I said.

Richard turned off the car and opened his door. Mom and the kids got out and I stayed put. She leaned down to look at me. "Christine?"

"Okay," I said, getting out. We walked to the door of the greenhouse and Richard held it open for us. The kids and I entered and Haley screamed at the sight. It was filled with kites of all shapes and colors, dangling paper butterflies, and hydrangea flowers sat in pots among the green plants and on the floor. I turned to look at Mom and Richard but they weren't behind us. I opened the door and their car was gone.

"Come on, Mom," Haley said, pulling me through the greenhouse. She broke loose from me and ran around the corner, anxious to see everything. Zach ran after her and I gaped at the flowers and kites. I rounded the corner and stopped, catching my breath at the sight of him.

"Merry Christmas, Christine."

Haley was holding his hand. "He did all this, Mom!"

He walked to me and my head felt light on my shoulders. "How did you —" I didn't even know where to begin.

"I went to your place last night. I was going to leave the necklace between the two doors but your father saw me and he came out to talk to me." I couldn't think of a time Richard wasn't in the house but it didn't matter now. "He put it under the tree for me." I touched the necklace and smiled, thinking of how Richard had played dumb all morning. "It was my grandmother's. My grandfather bought it a few years ago for their anniversary but didn't get the chance to give it to her. He wanted you to have it."

I was so confused. "Your grandfather?"

"It's a long story," he said, smiling. "He asked me recently if my heart beat faster at the thought of being in love and I had to say no. But that was then." He smiled and took another step closer. "I got a job this week," he said. "And it's a great job. It's a dream job, really. It offers me everything I want except one thing and of all the million ways to go — over there, or up there, or that way because it's the most obvious to everyone, I'm choosing this way. Or maybe it's choosing me. Regardless, this is the way I want to go." For a moment there was no sound but our breath. "If it's okay with you."

I smiled and felt my heart in my throat. "It's okay with me."

And on the day I learned Jason's name I kissed him.

EPILOGUE

The church bells ring as they have done at noon for the last eighty years. Is it cold today? I don't know. I haven't noticed. Some days are like that. One day, I'll relive these moments and remember everything, I hope. I step to the window and look outside. The sun is blazing a hole through the clouds and the sky is as clear and blue as I have ever seen. For some reason Jason's grandmother has been on my mind all morning. With thirty minutes to go I grab a bouquet of flowers off the table and run down the front steps to the street. In my rush I have forgotten that my dress is sleeveless and I'm not wearing a coat.

Horns blast and people yell as I cross the road and hurry through the town square. They think I'm a fool perhaps, or maybe they are shouts of wonder. I can hear Mom. "What are you doing?" she says, running after me. The air hits my lungs and I squint in the brightness of the day. I am surrounded by a blanket of white in the square and conscious of what I must look like running through it. My cheeks sting as I open the door to my car and for the first time today I realize it is cold. I lay the flowers on the seat beside me, start the engine, and drive the few blocks.

I leave the car running as I grab the flowers and close the door. A few inches of snow is on the ground so I hold up my dress and walk to the spot, placing the flowers atop the gray marble. "I got your flowers last year so I thought you should have these," I say, reading the words on Linda Marshall's tombstone: A wife of noble character who can find? She is worth far more than rubies. "You'd be proud of your men." Dennis's grave is not far from this spot but there's too much snow on the ground to cross to it. "Thank you!" I shout in that direction.

The car is warm as I slide back inside. I drive around the square and claim a spot in front of Wilson's. People watch as I run the two blocks and slip in through the side door. "Where did you go?" Mom asks. She is wearing a light teal dress with chiffon sleeves that hangs to just below her knee and is absolutely beautiful.

"I put flowers on Linda's grave," I say,

catching my breath.

"Today?"

"It's her day, Jeanette," Betty says, straightening the back of my dress. "She can do whatever she wants."

"Spoken like a true grandmother," Mom says. "The grandchildren can do no wrong!"

Mom sat Betty down on the day after Christmas last year and had a long tear-filled conversation with her. There were no feelings of resentment or bitterness that Mom had feared from Betty but only acceptance and more love than any of us expected. She's head-over-heels crazy about Zach and Haley and smashes my cheeks between her hands at least once a day to say, "Let me look at you. Beautiful. Just beautiful." She is the second grandmother I had always dreamed about.

Haley is wearing a soft pink dress with bright pink crinoline on the bottom that she says is "good for spinning." I haven't seen Zach since we arrived but I took pictures of him in his blue suit next to Haley at the house before we left. He held up two fingers behind her head and made a silly face. In a year when I've been busier than ever, the kids have been their happiest. I worried about going back to school but between their Grandma Betty, Jason, Gloria, Miriam, and Dolly watching them while I am in class they have thrived and even learned how to make cream cheese bear claws!

I work at Betty's three mornings a week and go to college the other two days and two evenings a week. I started in February and am on the fast track to receive my teaching degree in another eighteen months. Betty and Gloria helped me research every scholarship possible and Betty is paying the rest. "No, no, no," I said, the day she came over to talk about it.

She grabbed my face between her hands. "If Dennis had known he had this wonderful person in the world called a daughter he would have helped. Not at first. Not the way he was. But the way he became. He would have wanted to help you." I opened my mouth to speak but she talked over me. "And I am going to honor him by doing this."

I want to teach high school literature. Most people think I'm crazy to teach high schoolers but I loved my literature teacher. She developed my love for reading and I want to do that for other young people.

Brad found a job and moved to the next town over. He has called sporadically over the last year saying he wanted to see the kids but he never followed through with child support payments or interest. It's sad, really. He has no idea what he's missing.

Jason found a job at a small accounting firm in town and does the books for Wilson's. "Judy's always hated doing it," Marshall said. I met Judy for the second time last Christmas and she looked remarkably better than the first time I met her in my driveway. Jason and Marshall took me to her home and her husband hugged me so hard I could barely breathe.

Marshall and Gloria got married six months ago. "Why delay it?" he had asked. He moved into Gloria's house and cut back on his hours at work. Gloria and Miriam still meet for breakfast three times a week before going to Glory's Place and Miriam has now changed her order from a boiled egg to a poached one.

Tamara is here today. Her kids are with her and although she's still too thin, she's glowing. She graduated from the women's rescue mission's program and moved back to her hometown where she lives only a few blocks from her ex-husband and children. She has proven herself before the judge and her ex-husband and now shares joint custody of the children. Her life will never be what it was but she continues to take one step forward each day. It's the best that any of us can do.

I catch Mom wiping a tear from her cheek and I laugh. "Are you going to keep it together?"

"I'll be fine," she says.

The music swells and Richard leans toward us. "Come on, you two. It's time." I hug Richard and he kisses my cheek.

I reach for Mom and feel her melt into me. "I love you, Mom."

"I love you, too, sweet pea. You're more beautiful than I ever imagined." She pulls the veil over my face and holds out her arm.

Haley leads the way, sprinkling rose petals down the aisle. She dumps the last of them at the end and Zach smacks his head, watching her. My half sister, Lindsey, is a bridesmaid along with Renee, my longtime friend from Patterson's. They take their place at the front and I can see Jason, handsome and beaming in his tux. What started out as infatuation with him turned into something deeper and stronger than I could ever imagine. He is smart and compassionate and every time he's with the kids, he's a natural. I don't even know when I started thinking of them as his children. They still call him Jason but I know it's only a matter of time before we're back from the honeymoon and living in the same house together as a family that they claim him as their dad. Mom clutches my hand on her arm and together we walk down the aisle.

I smile as I walk, amazed at the faces in the church. When I stand back and look at the people in my life I continue to be surprised and grateful. There have been so many moments in the last year — everyday, commonplace, but glistening moments that pass through my mind. There's nothing sensational, cinematic, or mysterious about them; they would never make it on the evening news or daytime talk shows but they all point to the same conclusion — that we are all here to help one another move the boulder.

That is the secret of the treasure.